What the Critics say about...

OATH OF SEDUCTION

Winner of Romantic Times Magazine's Reviewers Choice Award for Best Small Press Futuristic Book of 2002.

"I highly recommend this book to anyone who enjoys their romance hot. A 6'7" psychic alien cop with black hair and piercing blue eyes who wants to make all your fantasies come true...what's not to like?" – *B. Small for Paranormal Romance Reviews*

"For a sizzling read guaranteed to raise your temperature, I recommend Marly Chance's OATH OF SEDUCTION: SEDUCING SHARON." – *Terrie Figueroa, Romance Reviews Today*

OATH OF CHALLENGE

Nominated for the SilverMoon Chalice Award for Best Fantasy Book of 2002.

"This highly anticipated sequel to 'Oath Of Seduction' was well worth the wait. Kate and Tair's incendiary reaction to one another will keep readers glued to the pages eager for the outcome of this battle of the sexes...If you enjoyed 'Oath Of Seduction' go and buy 'Oath Of Challenge' you won't regret it." — *B Small, Paranormal Romance Reviews*

"This is the second book in Marly Chance's Oath series and I highly recommend both. This was a fun read from the beginning and I couldn't put it down. My only wish is that there were more books written by this author." – *Laura Lane for Sensual Romance Reviews*

WICKED WISHES

With Stephanie Burke and Joanna Wylde nominated for the Readers Choice Golden Rose Award for Best Anthology of 2002.

"Three little wishes, three magnificent tales! This is an extremely well put together anthology and the authors compliment each other very nicely. All are very romantic, all are very hot! If you like fantasy and science fiction blended with love, you're sure to delight in the anthology known as Wicked Wishes. And OH how wicked..." – *Amy L. Turpin, Timeless Tales*

Discover for yourself why readers can't get enough of the multiple award-winning publisher Ellora's Cave. Whether you prefer e-books or paperbacks, be sure to visit EC on the web at www.ellorascave.com for an erotic reading experience that will leave you breathless.

WWW.ELLORASCAVE.COM

Oath of Seduction: Seducing Sharon
An Ellora's Cave Publication, October 2004

Ellora's Cave Publishing, Inc.
1337 Commerce Drive Suite 13
Stow OH 44224

Previously published in 2003.

Edited by Martha Punches, Cris Brashear, and Tina Engler
Cover art by Syneca

OATH OF SEDUCTION: SEDUCING SHARON

By Marly Chance

Dedicated to my family, for always believing

Chapter One

It seemed like a good idea at the time. Now all of these years later, she had to laugh at the sheer perversity of fate. He was sex personified. She was just a small town librarian.

Standing in front of her, dressed in a black silk shirt and leather pants, he had to be six feet seven inches of sculpted, mouth-watering, sexy muscle. He was the kind of guy mothers warned daughters to avoid, and best friends advised, "Sure, enjoy the ride while you can, but he's gonna break your heart eventually."

His hair, cropped close to his head military-style, was pitch black. His face was all masculine angles. He was beautiful in a warrior kind of way. He looked about thirty-five years old, with quite a few of those years tough ones. This was no pretty-boy, sensitive, in-touch-with-his-feelings man. This guy was total danger. He was completely out of her league.

She was pretty much cotton gowns, a good book, and a cheery nightlight. He was sweaty, forbidden, no boundaries sex in the dark. As her gaze met his fully for the first time, she saw that they were a searing, penetrating blue. Within that gaze, she saw the blue flame of intense desire and possession. He wanted her, no doubt of that, but even more frightening, his gaze roamed her body as if he had already claimed it. Repeatedly. Intimately.

Sharon felt like she'd stepped off of a cliff. Her heart was pounding, her skin was flushed, and she had an impulse to scream. She dropped her gaze to the carpeting in pure panic.

This had been a really big mistake. Maybe doing her duty and registering had not been a good idea. Maybe she'd just paste a smile on her face, look him in the eye and say, "Look, I know we're supposed to be getting engaged, but could you maybe find another fiancée? I can't have screaming sex with you. I'm just a librarian, for goodness sake. I'm not really adventurous. I don't really want to live on another planet or meld minds or whatever alien activities are required. I'll just be running along now..." With a deep breath, she raised her gaze to his and felt the words become trapped in her throat.

He was smiling. In fact, he looked on the verge of laughter. The sudden amusement softened his features a little, making him more approachable. She wasn't fooled. It made him even more dangerous.

With a little annoyed sniff, she squared her shoulders. Okay, she was scared, terrified even, but if he was going to keep laughing at her, he was going to be sorry—she'd find a way to make him pay. She took a deep breath. Her hands clinched and she aggressively leaned toward him. Her knees might be knocking, but she would show him that she was not afraid of any big, smirking, sexy, annoying guy. Ever. He'd better understand right now that she was no pushover.

* * * * *

Liken looked at the little beauty standing so scared and defiant in front of him, and felt his heart rejoice. She was perfect. Her five-foot, eight-inch frame was practically vibrating with nerves and outrage. She was both beautiful and courageous. He appreciated the beauty, but she would need the courage in the times to come. She was fighting his effect on her now, but that would change. He would make sure of it. First, though, he had to get his own arousal under control.

She had long, black hair that dropped just past her shoulders. Seeing it in person, rather than telepathically, made him ache with the need to run his hands through it. He wanted that hair spread across his pillow. Or better yet, across every inch of his body. Her eyes were like *mer* stones, deep green and seemingly lit from within. Her face was not classically Shimerian beautiful. The mouth was a little too full, the nose a little too pert. The overall effect on his senses, however, was devastating.

He wanted that face looking at him with desire, with need. He wanted those full lips swollen and tender from his mating or rather, from his lovemaking. When on Earth, think like a human, he chided himself.

Yet even with that thought, his gaze drifted down the rest of her body. Full breasts, the nipples hardening beneath his gaze, were heaving with her rapid breaths. The tips were little defiant points underneath the traditional white blouse. It was fitted to her body, but not tightly. The scooped neckline showed the upper swell of creamy curves. He could tell she wore no undergarment, and those tight nipples were stiff and visible.

Going lower, he saw a small waist, tapering outward to full hips. He felt his hands flex with the need to sink his fingers into those curves and pull her toward him. The white ceremonial skirt fell all the way to the ground. What would those long legs look like? And what would they feel like wrapped around his hips?

Calling on all his discipline, he again raised his gaze to hers and felt the jolt to his soul. She would be his. He had no doubt. Attempting to ease her fear, he said, "Do not fear me, Sharon. I am merely invoking our oath. I am your pactmate, Liken da'Kamon. I would never harm you."

"I'm not afraid of you," she said a little too quickly. They both wondered if she meant to convince him or herself. "Why would I be afraid? This is just the ceremony. I don't think we'll be at all compatible. I think we should just say our words and then when it's over, you can go your way and I'll go mine. At the end of the knowing period, we'll just meet back here and file incompatible."

"You are mine. You will leave with me." The words were out of his mouth without any thought. Seeing her eyes widen, he fell back on Shimerian strategy. Timing was crucial to gaining any objective, particularly with females. "We will speak no more, Sharon, until after the ceremony. We should not be speaking now. Go to the Pactmaker and wait for me." With those words, he turned and walked to the other side of the room.

He might as well have said "Get thee to a nunnery!" like some classic Shakespearean character. Sharon, shocked speechless at his arrogance, stood there until she felt a slight tug on her arm.

Turning, she looked into her friend Kate's face and said, "I am *so* out of here. No way can I go through with this. How dare he order me over to the Pactmaker like I was some child to command? What was I thinking? Kate, we have to find a way to get me out of here."

Kate, her friend since elementary school, knew her only too well. "Shar, what did he say to you? You look scared to death. Did he threaten you or something?"

Turning back toward the other side of the room, Kate leveled a glower toward the Shimerian males gathered there. Finding the one who had frightened Sharon, she gave him a look meant to kill him on sight. To her disappointment, he merely raised an eyebrow.

The male he was in conversation with, however, grinned widely at her and gave a mocking little nod with his head. He was arrogantly gorgeous and his hot gaze, as it raked her body, felt incredibly familiar. He looked enough like Sharon's looming problem to be his brother.

She felt a shot of unease, and immediately turned her back on him. Shaking off the disturbing feelings, she asked Sharon, "What happened?"

Sharon, wrestling her own demons, missed her friend's exchange with the other warrior. She shrugged and said, "No, he didn't threaten me exactly. He more or less told me to shut up and go stand by the Pactmaker. I can't do it, Kate. I know when we registered we thought we were doing the right thing. But now, I'm freaked."

She struggled for calm as she remembered the beginning of this mess. "You know, when you're eighteen, you think you know everything. You have such high ideals. Registering seemed so simple. It was my duty. All of us felt like that. I don't think any of us really thought about what would happen if the Shimerian male showed up to fulfill the pact. I mean, what are the odds? Only about one in twenty thousand is ever called to fulfill the pact. I know it's my duty as a human to go through the ceremony and observe the customs, but I don't think I can."

Kate, feeling sorry for her friend, felt helpless. What could she say? All of them had registered in an idealistic rush of patriotism and duty without really counting the potential costs. Now her friend, the girl she'd literally grown up with and loved like a sister, was being legally and morally tied to an alien being who might remove her from all she held dear. Sharon would have to be intimate with him. She was such an innocent in so many ways. It was frightening and upsetting. Sharon didn't have many choices unless…"Have you really thought out all the options?"

With a shake of her head, Sharon said, "There wasn't really time to think. The two Pactmaker reps showed up at my door in uniform and told me to come with them. They didn't even let me grab my purse. The whole thing scared the crap out of me! I just couldn't believe it was happening, you know?"

She could feel her body begin to shake as reality really hit. "I mean, it crossed my mind when I turned twenty-nine last week that the claiming age would be over in a year. But, it just seemed so unlikely. They brought me to the city pactbuilding and gave me these clothes to put on. Now I've got twenty minutes to figure out what I'm going to do. I don't even know how they knew to get you here. Since I don't have any immediate family, I guess they picked you to stand with me."

It seemed logical, but Kate knew they needed to focus on what was happening now. She was the lawyer here. She ought to be able to fix this situation. She had to find a way to help Sharon. "Well, we can talk about the fun experience I had with the pact reps some other time. Right now, we've got to figure out what you are going to do. You only have three options: Seduction, Challenge, or Capture. Each has its own set of rules and problems. How much do you remember of the customs course?"

Mind racing, Sharon searched her memory. "If I choose seduction, we recite vows, go to his planet, and then live together for three weeks. He..." Her voice faltered a bit but she spoke up deliberately after only a second, "follows the Courtship Rules of Seduction. That means he's allowed certain intimacies with me at certain times. Kind of like baseball...first base, second, like that. He can go further than the prescribed intimacies only with my permission."

Sharon felt her panic rising as she tried frantically to remember what they had been taught. "God, how long before total intimacy, Kate?! I can't remember!"

Kate thought back and then said, "Damn it, they wouldn't give me time to get my copy of your paperwork." Her expression indicated someone would pay for that fact later. "I can't remember. Maybe two or three days at the most."

Three days. It wasn't long enough. Sharon didn't think two or three years would be long enough to make her comfortable with the idea of sleeping with that man. Still, at worst, after a few weeks of living together, she could file for incompatibility and never see him again. "What about Challenge?"

Kate sighed and said with careful calm, "You recite the ceremony and make the oath, but you are basically challenging him to seduce you into staying with him. You have to cooperate with anything he orders you to do sexually, but you can ultimately refuse to have intercourse with him. He can keep you for two weeks. It's his goal in that time to overcome your objections and make you want to stay. If you give in and actually have intercourse, you are ineligible for an incompatibility filing. I don't know, though, Sharon. Shimerian males are supposed to be so dominant in bed..."

Sharon thought of Liken being able to do whatever he wanted for two full weeks except intercourse. She shuddered. There was excitement at the thought, too, but she didn't feel that she could challenge him sexually with her level of experience. She'd only had two lovers, both of whom had been rather dull and unimaginative. Sex had been warmly intimate, but not exactly earthshaking.

This guy was a walking Kama Sutra. She didn't think she could hold her own in that kind of fight and come out on top for sure. "Nope. No way. He's way out of my league. That only leaves Capture. I'm leaning toward that. I say the words and all, but then I get to leave. I have one full day's head start. If I can evade him for one month, I can file incompatible then." She was starting to feel calmer at the thought.

Kate frowned. "Yeah, but if he catches you, you're in a fix. He gets the rest of the month of full sexual obedience. He can do anything he likes, short of seriously hurting you. He doesn't need permission at any time for anything, including intercourse. He has to be guided by your sexual likes and dislikes, but he doesn't have to play fair at all. The rumor is that they're telepathic or mentally gifted or something."

Kate's voice caught as her imagination leapt at the possibilities. "I don't know what that means exactly, but he can probably read your mind. If he picks up on something you would like, but would never admit to liking, he'll use it ruthlessly. He can't actually make you do anything that would be sexually repulsive, but he would push your boundaries pretty hard I'd imagine. We've all heard rumors and stories about the Shimerians' incredible sexuality. It might be pretty intense. You're not that experienced. It would be pretty frightening for you."

Frightening? The thought was enough to make her want to run from the room right now. There had to be some way to deal with this situation. Thinking hard, she quietly said, "But if I break the oath..."

Both women sighed and looked away. There were legal penalties for not fulfilling oaths-"long years in a penal institution with some very uncomfortable companions" kind of penalties. Besides, the guilt and shame of it would be awful. Each woman registering had made an oath of their own free will at the request of their government.

The Shimerian population was in trouble. They had a great disproportion of males. There were not enough females to mate with males and make families. Of the children born, a large percentage was male. It was a downward spiral, and the Earth government had agreed to help, ending with the signing of the Friendship Treaty.

Earth provided potential mates for Shimerians. In return, Shimerian resources and technology were fully available to Earth. Already, amazing cures for some of the worst Earth diseases had resulted from the cooperative knowledge provided by Shimerian scientists to Earth scientists. All kinds of positive advances were taking place.

The Earth government, making clear it was not prostituting its people, agreed to provide a register of potential mates and carefully agreed upon Courtship Laws. Since the Shimerian males' version of courtship leaned toward kidnapping and seduction, the Earth government had been very specific that the program would be voluntary and follow prescribed rules. If, after the knowing period, the Earth female did not want to continue the union, she could file legal paperwork that the union was incompatible and should be dissolved.

When the treaty had been signed some eighty years ago, there was hesitation by Earth females and only a few actually became Shimerian mates. However, as the positive breakthroughs in technology and medicine began to become widely felt, the Shimerian government pushed hard for a public relations program in colleges to promote registering.

These "culture classes" explained the process in glowing terms and encouraged young women to register. The classes had a very idealistic slant with just enough excitement to entice. "Help your fellow human beings and Shimerians, too," they persuaded, "while having an adventure."

More Earth females registered and were mated. Then, rumors began to surface about Shimerian men and their sexual abilities. Women spoke with sighs of their physical attributes, but a lot of information remained unknown. There was just enough mystery to intrigue and entice even the most hardheaded of women. More and more Earth females registered.

After a while, the overwhelming response meant that for every twenty thousand Earth women registered, only one would actually be called to Oath. Most would go on to fall in love with a man on Earth. When she married, or reached age thirty, her name would be removed from the register with thanks from her government for her willingness to serve.

Sharon sighed. Breaking Oath wasn't really an option. She had made a promise to her world, and for that matter, to his world. She might be a lot of things, but she wasn't the kind of person to break her word.

Kate's eyes were soft with sympathy and worry. "What are you going to do?"

"Make the best of it, I guess. Take the oath. Go with him to Shimeria. It's only three weeks, right? And he's not a total troll either. So I'll get to know him. Then, I'll come home and file incompatible. My life is here. Maybe my job isn't the greatest. Maybe my little life isn't the most exciting. But it's *mine*. I'm not giving it up and moving off planet for some guy." She was going for defiant, but her words came out shaky instead.

Kate knew that was her cue to lighten things up. "Not a total troll, huh? Now there's an understatement. That man is *hot*. You'll be doing your duty *and* getting great sex. At least I assume it'll be great if he's as good as he looks!"

"Exactly." Sharon began to smile a little as her sense of humor rose to the surface. "Besides, a little interplanetary nookie won't kill me. They're basically humanoid. Their society is very similar to ours, just a little more advanced. It's pretty male-dominated, but I guess I can live with that for a few weeks. I don't know about the telepathy thing but I don't think they can read minds all the time or anything. I guess I'll find out…"

Determined to keep smiling and make the best of it, she headed toward the Pactmaker. "Come on," she called to Kate. "Might as well get it over with. We wouldn't want Mr. Tall, Dark, and Arrogant to get his drawers in a twist."

Laughing at that image, the two women headed to the other side of the room. Shimerian male heads turned at the sound. Watching the two beautiful women appreciatively, hearing their laughter, many of them felt a little envious of Liken. Liken, on the other hand, was feeling too eager for the ceremony to pay much attention. His brother Tair, sensing that eagerness, had to laugh.

He said mockingly, "You should have claimed her a year ago, Liken. Then maybe you would not be so impatient today."

Liken shook his head. "You know I was giving her time. She will be making a lot of changes. Best that she grew restless with her own life before facing Shimerian marriage. It will be difficult for her."

Liken thought of his cautious little librarian's reaction to his culture and mentally grimaced. She would not react well. There were good reasons for keeping Shimerian ways a secret from prospective mates.

"You are sure that she has no idea of the merging and linking? We are taught to be careful, but there have been some rumors on Earth from time to time." Tair had heard some pretty outrageous things, although some of them had some truth to them.

"No, I do not think so. She seems afraid of me in an emotional and physical sense, but I have not brushed her mind with mine yet. Except for my initial recognition a year ago. My mind touched hers then, but only briefly."

Tair shook his head at the thought of what his brother would need to explain. Humans, especially females, could react very strangely to the oddest things. His voice was dry. "Just be sure to secure her. It is quite convenient that my pactmate is her best friend. I think Kate will be much more amiable when I invoke the Oath if she knows Sharon is happy."

"So, I am to ease your way?" Liken said with a half-smile. He nearly snorted at the thought. Kate would challenge Tair at every turn. She was perfect for him. "I believe your knowing period will not be that simple. The look she sent me earlier could have felled me. I do not think your pactmate is the sweet, gentle type."

Tair's dark eyes gleamed with laughter. "Now what would I do with sweet and gentle?"

Suddenly, the Pactmaker, a rather small man dressed in his ceremonial robes of black and white stepped forward to address those gathered. "Will Liken da'Kamon and Sharon Glaston please step forward to take the Oath?" There was a murmur throughout the room at the sound of his words.

Most of the Shimerian males present were single and waiting anxiously to make arrangements for invoking their own oaths. They were lined along the wall waiting for their turn with the official Pactmaker representatives. All were dressed casually in different colors and styles of pants, shirts, and boots, but one thing was common to each and every one. There was a palpable sense of impatience and sheer male power exuding from each of the males. They were eager to conclude their business, but they were curious about the oath ceremony. For many of them, this ceremony would be the first one they had seen. Coming so close to their own pactmaking arrangements, the ceremony gained a certain significance.

Liken strode to where the Pactmaker waited. Sharon took the last steps remaining between them and came to stand at his side. Tair stood in the background to Liken's left, while Kate waited on Sharon's right. Tair's gaze met Kate's fuming gaze for one long moment before they turned to watch the other couple.

The next twenty minutes of the ceremony were a blur. Sharon heard the droning voice of the Pactmaker and responded whenever prompted. The actual words seemed to be coming from a great distance and she couldn't really grasp the meanings. The only thing she could hear clearly was the pounding of her own heart, which seemed to be coming out of her chest.

She kept her gaze on the Pactmaker and kept repeating to herself silently, "Liken, his name is Liken. I'm gonna have sex with the guy, so I should try to remember his name. He's an alien. I wonder if sex is the same? I'm not gonna get hysterical. I can do this. I have to do this. It's no big deal. It will be fine. I can do this..." Sharon hoped that if she repeated the words over and over again, she might convince herself that she was doing the right thing.

She could feel the heat of Liken's tall presence standing strong and still beside her. Only once did his big body grow stiff with tension. The Pactmaker repeated the words, "Your choice, my dear. You need to state it clearly...which oath do you choose, Seduction, Challenge or Capture?" The room was silent as everyone present waited for her reply.

She took a deep breath. Her mind spun with confusion like a top. What should she do? What could she do? She said in a quaking voice that was nearly inaudible, "Seduction." She felt ridiculous and mortified to even say the word. Feeling the tension leave him, she hoped it was the right choice. Putting some strength into her voice, she said more firmly, "I choose Seduction."

Sharon heard Liken state the rest of his vow in a strong, masculine voice. She knew he was speaking English, but she couldn't seem to absorb what he was saying. She felt disconnected from the entire scene.

Finally, the ceremony was complete. Liken held out his hand and said her name softly, then a little louder. "Sharon…"

Sharon suddenly realized he was waiting for her to put her hand in his. Trembling, she reached out. The hand that caught hers was warm and strong. She nearly shuddered at the contact. It felt good and scary at the same time. As his thumb caressed the softness of her hand in a soothing motion, she realized her own hand was trembling.

He gave her hand a gentle tug, making her raise her gaze to his face for the first time since the ceremony began. His smile was both satisfied and teasing. "You will be fine. You can do this…a little interplanetary nookie won't kill you…"

Sharon gasped softly as she heard him repeat her earlier words. "You were spying on us!" She felt angry and embarrassed. Her mind worked frantically, trying to remember what else she and Kate had said earlier.

With relief he watched the color come back into her face. She had gone pale and trembling during the ceremony, but anger was bringing her back to life. "Shimerian hearing is exceptional, *sherree* . Something you might want to remember in the future. We have all kinds of interesting qualities I'm sure you'll enjoy."

His smile broadened. "It's time to go to the portal. Say your farewell to your friend." He gently turned her in the direction of Kate and shook hands with the Pactmaker. Accepting the congratulations of the gathered males, he kept an eye on Sharon.

Sharon walked the few feet to Kate, who had angry tears in her eyes. She hated to see Kate so upset when there was nothing either of them could do to change things. She tried for a light tone. "It's only a few weeks right? I'll be coming back to file the papers and then it will be over. Life will be just the same as it was." Even she could hear the doubt in her voice.

Kate agreed immediately, a little desperately. "That's right. I'll meet you here when you get back. You'll be fine. We'll go to

O'Tooles and have a little celebration. Get silly and drunk. Dance and make fools of ourselves." Thoughts of all the terrible things that could happen to Sharon were running through her mind, but she knew it wouldn't help Sharon to hear them. Sharon needed to believe it would be okay.

Sharon rallied. "I can tell you what it's like to sleep with the stud of the universe."

Kate gave a weak laugh. "Sleep? I don't see you getting much sleep." They smiled at each other. Hugging her close, Kate whispered in her ear. "Give him hell. Make him treat you right. If he doesn't, we'll both kick his ass."

Kate felt a touch on her shoulder. Startled, she looked back to find the Shimerian male who had made her so nervous earlier. He was even more gorgeous at close range. "What?" Her tone was hostile.

His grin only widened. "She will be fine. My brother will be good to her. They will be good together."

Her chin went up higher. "Yes, she will be fine. Because if she isn't, your brother will be sorry. You'll both be sorry. I'm a lawyer. I'm not threatening to sue you. I'm telling you my profession so you'll understand what a mean bitch I can be. I don't worry about playing fair. I just win. You understand?"

She looked ready to attack him physically if her friend came to any injury. His dark eyes gleamed with appreciation and some secret amusement. "I understand more than you think, *sheka* . And I look forward to playing with you." With those easy words, he turned and walked away.

Kate could only stare at him as his statements registered. He wasn't a bit intimidated by her. She wasn't used to that kind of reaction when she went into her "dangerous bitch mode." It was very effective, especially with men.

Sharon laughed. She couldn't help it. "I can't believe it…you threatened him and he seemed to enjoy it." Genuine amusement drained away a lot of her tension.

Kate made a small sound of disbelief. "I hate him." Shaking off all thoughts of the intergalactic jerk, she hugged Sharon one last time, hard. "Take care of yourself. I'll see you soon." Then, before she could get too emotional, she turned and walked out of the room.

Sharon watched Kate until she disappeared. Her heart sank as she realized that her final link to Earth had just walked out that door.

Chapter Two

Feeling lost and alone, Sharon looked around the pactroom. Liken was heading toward her, accepting congratulations as he went. Reaching her, he grabbed her hand again and started pulling her across the room toward the exit. She struggled to keep up with his long strides as they finally reached the hallway. Taking a quick right and then a left, he pulled her into a deserted office and backed her up against the wall.

Startled, she gasped, pulling her hand from his. Bringing both hands up against his chest, she pushed against him as he crowded her. He wasn't actually touching her, but there were only inches separating them.

Taking her chin, he raised her face so that their gaze met. "I cannot wait any longer." There was urgency in his voice and something suspiciously like need.

Sharon, feeling a wave of pure panic, choked out, "Don't!"

"It is my right..." Bringing both hands to cradle her face gently, but firmly, he lowered his mouth toward hers.

She expected a hard, devouring kiss. Instead, he played teasingly with her lips, lightly touching then withdrawing, then touching again. Her lips tingled and she felt like all the air was being drawn from her lungs. He kissed one corner, softly touching it with his tongue, then licked outward along the rest of her mouth. The soft wetness of his tongue, the gentle firmness of his lips made her feel restless, unsatisfied. She felt helpless under the gentle assault. His tongue kept inching closer along the seam of her mouth, seeking entrance.

"Open for me, *sherree* . Let me taste you..." His voice was sinfully soft and beguiling, as he continued luring her.

She could feel her lips parting with a sigh. He took immediate advantage, breaching her lips gently and then finding her tongue with his own. With that discovery, he ran his tongue along hers, penetrating her, mimicking the act both their bodies craved. He continued to thrust gently until her tongue began to parry. With her response, the kiss changed entirely.

Like a match thrown on gasoline, his body moved forward into hers. The hands on her face moved down to her shoulders and then slid around her body between her and the wall. He stroked her like a cat and then used those hands to pull her forward against the muscular length of his body.

Her nipples tightened. She felt the moistness between her legs. He felt so good against her. Every inch of him was hard. Cradling his erection between her thighs, she rubbed and felt a burst of pleasure. With a moan, she started to press herself even closer. With a moan of his own, he pushed his hips forward, pressing upwards hard and then teasingly easing back.

Then, she felt something else entirely. Like the tickling of a feather, his mind brushed softly against hers. The realization stunned her. Before she could react, the touch grew firmer. His mind was pressing against hers like their bodies were pressed against each other. She froze, every muscle locking up. Her hands, which had somehow been clinging to his shoulders like a lifeline, squeezed hard in protest. Pushing her head back against the wall, she said tightly, "Let me go. Now!"

Liken searched her face as he tried to bring his breathing under control. God, she was beautiful. She felt like pure pleasure under his hands. Every cell in his body ached to disregard her words and take her. His cock was hard, throbbing. Calling on all his discipline, he reminded himself that she was essentially a virgin when it came to Shimerian ways. Purposefully gentling his hands, he rubbed her back as he moved his hands up to her shoulders. He would have her soon, but he had to proceed with care.

"You are right, Sharon. We need to get to the portal. There will be time enough for such pleasures later." He could barely wait as images of the coming pleasure flashed through his mind.

Sharon blinked as if coming out of a daze. He looked hungry enough to forget about waiting and just take her, rules or no rules. Her cheeks began to burn with color and she said, "We are not doing this again. I don't know you. I'm not sure I even like you. You can't just kiss me whenever you want. We need to set some guidelines here..." Her words faltered as his face grew harsh.

"You would go back on your oath?" He felt angry that she was threatening it when he knew she would do no such thing.

Sharon was surprised at his vehemence. "No, no I didn't say that," she said quickly. "I just need some time to get used to things, okay? I went to work at the library this morning. This afternoon, I took an Oath I had nearly forgotten about and didn't really expect to have to do. You yanked me out of the room and started kissing me. We need to slow down here..."

Liken shook his head. "There is no slowing down, only moving forward from here. Any intimacy we have shared can be repeated at your will or mine. I can take further intimacies at prescribed times in the days to come, but never forget: once you allow something, I can do it again at my choosing."

Her eyes looked angry. "Gee, thanks for the patience and understanding, big guy."

His voice gentled. "I can be patient and understanding, *sherree*. But I am also a demanding person. That cannot be helped. How can you expect to share such pleasure with me, and then ask me to forego it? I am merely being honest with you."

Sharon shook her head. "Whatever. Let's just get to the portal. I'm tired of being surprised and confused. Of not knowing what to expect from one moment to the next. I hate surprises. I hate this. Let's just go and get this over with."

Liken leaned down and placed a hard kiss against her mouth. It was over with before she could object. Taking her hand again in his, he strode out of the room and down the hallway. As they approached the lobby of the massive building, Sharon saw a sign indicating the portal for Shimeria was down two flights of stairs and to the left.

As they walked, she realized suddenly that all she had were the clothes she was wearing. She wasn't exactly prepared for interplanetary travel. She tried to slow her steps as she asked Liken, "What about my clothes, my things? I didn't even think about leaving right after the Oath."

Liken kept them moving forward as he said, "All has been prepared. I've known about you for a year, Sharon. You have all you need at my dwelling."

"Ohhh. Okay. Sure." She couldn't seem to focus. She wondered if her system had sustained too many shocks for one day. The pact reps, the oath, him, his kisses, his touch...

She needed to focus her thoughts and think about this whole thing in a more orderly, logical fashion.

As they walked, she considered what had happened in the deserted office minutes ago, trying to be more objective. It had been exciting. He had been forceful, but gentle. Things might not be so bad. That mind thing was weird, but he had stopped immediately. He might be predatory in some ways, but he had backed off when she asked.

She sighed unconsciously. There was nothing she could do to change things. Logically, it was childish and unproductive to sulk or fight with him constantly. She would do as she had told Kate. Make the best of it.

With a conciliatory smile, she told him, "I'm sorry. I don't know or remember much about Shimeria and its customs. The one class I had was years..." She stopped as what he said suddenly hit her. "A year? What do you mean you've known about me for a year?"

They had reached the portal and this was one discussion he hoped to avoid for a time. He used the distraction of the busy room as an excuse to not answer. There were Shimerians streaming through one portal on the right. They were showing ID cards to customs officers as they passed.

Sharon and Liken approached their own checkpoint for customs. Liken turned and handed her a Shimerian ID card. It had her name on it. She studied it in silence. Obviously, he really had made preparations for her. As Liken handed the officer his ID card and responded to his questions, Sharon waited impatiently. She wasn't going to drop this discussion.

The customs officer handed Liken back his card and then asked for hers. With a bureaucratic look of apathy that was recognizable on any planet, he glanced at her card and then handed it back. With a disinterested smile, he waved them forward. Sharon went a few more steps and then halted in awe.

She had been so focused on Liken that she had not noticed her surroundings. She gulped as she took in the two portals for the first time. She had never traveled off planet or seen one of the portals. Each portal structure was at least two stories tall. Made like an oval gate, the metal was unrecognizable. There were lever-like devices to the side that appeared to operate the opening and closing of the gate. Inside the open gate, was dense, flat blackness.

It would be like stepping into nothingness. She watched the other portal as Shimerians coming to Earth stepped through unharmed. They didn't appear to be missing any appendages.

Liken, remembering his awe and momentary fear when seeing the portal the first time, waited for her to begin walking again. In this situation at least, he would give her time.

Reminding herself logically that Liken had obviously survived it, she started walking. At the edge of the portal he stopped and looked down at her. "Sharon, we cannot go at the same time. Unpledged females such as yourself must arrive on Shimeria alone to signify you are coming of your own free will. I will go first. Once I disappear, step through."

She pulled her gaze away from the portal to look up at him. "You trust me to step through after you?" she said with some surprise.

"Of course," he said with a smile. "You have courage and will not break your oath. Besides, my mind brushed yours. I have some sense of what you feel. You have been through much today, but you are curious, too. I will be waiting on the other side, *sherree*. Once there, I will satisfy your curiosity. I will satisfy you in any way you desire." With a wink and a quick kiss, he stepped through. With one step, he was gone and Sharon was left staring into the dense blackness of the portal.

For about ten seconds, she considered proving him wrong. With a sigh, and a muttered "I *desire* to stay here, Mr. Tall, Dark, and Know-It-All" under her breath, she stepped through.

She had made her choice. What the hell.

Chapter Three

For a moment, time stood still. Sharon felt a numbing blackness pressing in all around her. Her lungs seized; she couldn't breath. Her body felt as if she was falling, but she couldn't see or hear anything. Then, before true panic could take hold, light blinded her and she felt air rush into her lungs.

She was standing on the other side of the gate. Liken quickly gathered her close, whispering softly, "Well done, *sherree*. The disorientation will pass in just a second. It is a little overwhelming at first. Just concentrate on your breathing. In, out, deep breaths…"

Sharon looked up at him and said, "I…don't…like…portals. I've just…decided." She gave him a weak smile. "That sucked." His arms felt warm and the weight of them around her felt comforting.

He laughed. "You will be fine." Gesturing with one arm to the room around them, he said more seriously, "Welcome to my world, Sharon." His voice was quiet, rather solemn.

Sharon looked around her. She didn't really know what she expected, but the room around her looked pretty much like the room they had just left. Even the bored customs officer looked the same, only his sheer size and that vague power the Shimerians seemed to have in common gave him away. He was gesturing with one arm for her to proceed. His voice carried strained politeness, although the undertone of impatience was clear. "Progress forward, *Isshal* . More passengers await."

Sharon's mouth dropped open. What an insulting planet! She heard herself say with quiet dignity, "No problem, asshole."

Liken gave a choked laugh. "He did not call you an asshole. You insult him, *sherree*. He was merely addressing you formally. *Isshal* is the Shimerian equivalent of ma'am."

The transport officer was looking at her with a combination of anger and shock. His face had gone red.

Sharon felt her own color rise along with her embarrassment. "I'm so sorry. Really. I'm new here and I thought…"

Liken laughed and said, "It is okay, Sharon. Let us move along."

She let him pull her through the room. She definitely wasn't on Earth anymore, no matter how familiar everything looked. Of course, she had expected something totally different for her first experience of another planet. Feeling somewhat disappointed, she followed Liken up two flights of stairs and into a large lobby area.

Liken, sensing her disappointment, said, "It is a way to help with the disorientation. Making both buildings look essentially the same makes the drama of the voyage a little more mundane. It is supposed to be calming. Being on a new world for the first time can be somewhat overwhelming. If you will notice, the signs in this building are in various languages. The top is Shimerian, but underneath are several Earth languages as well as other planetary tongues. There are differences here, but after the shock of the trip, it is best absorbed slowly."

Understanding the common sense of his remarks, Sharon remained silent as they walked through the lobby. There were no windows, just the bland walls of an office building, although they looked pink. She knew other people had to have left the building before them, but she couldn't see any exit doors. She let Liken guide her toward one of the walls. As they moved, she thought to ask, "What time is it here?" It had been late afternoon when they left Earth.

"It is early moonstime. Ahhh, I believe about eight o'clock in the evening, by your time. I should probably remind you that Shimerian moonslight is different." Liken pushed a large button on the wall. She watched in amazement as part of the wall opened and slid inside itself.

"Different how…" The words had no sooner left her mouth than she could tell he had opened a sliding door. Outside the building was a city street, similar to the streets where they had left. There were no vehicles or modes of transportation visible. There were offices made of rocklike material similar to brick, but they were glowing in the moonlight. The light was pure silver. Looking up, she saw two large silvery moons overhead right next to each other.

Liken saw where she was looking in the evening sky. "Those are Tilus and Noman," he explained.

Stepping out into the light, she noticed her skin glimmering as if she had been dusted in mother of pearl. It was strange. Liken's skin remained the same color. "Why am I shiny?" It was bizarre, but kind of neat.

He said, "I do not know. I am sure there is a scientific reason, but all humans experience the same thing in moonslight. It is very attractive. Some Shimerian women even try to emulate it by applying glittering powder. It never looks the same." He could feel his body harden at the sight of her glowing in the moonslight. She looked delicate and beautiful.

"So, there are native Shimerian women here?" she asked. She had seen women travelers paired with some of the Shimerian men back in the portal room. The women had the same dark hair and intense charisma of their male counterparts.

"Yes, but very few." He sounded a little sad. Then, his mouth lifted in a smile, "Of course, if there were more, I might never have met you, *sherree*."

Visions of him kissing another woman as he had kissed her in the empty office came to mind. She didn't like the thought. She didn't like the feeling of jealousy that accompanied it, either. Resolutely pushing those thoughts aside, she asked, "How do we get to your home?"

Liken watched the changing expressions on her face. That brief flash of jealousy pleased him immensely. His little librarian was feeling possessive already. Things were progressing nicely. Not wanting her to guess at his happiness, he pointed to a sign that read "shimvehi." There was a staircase leading downward next to it. "It is like your subway. We will be using it to get to *our* home, Sharon."

Shrugging her shoulders, she followed him down the staircase. Each step seemed to be difficult. Feeling strangely lethargic, she wondered about interplanetary jetlag. At the bottom of the stairs, there was something resembling a subway train. People, some native Shimerian, some obviously from other planets, were gathering in lines to get into what looked like subway cars. The individual cars had seats like benches inside where people sat.

There were no lone, unescorted females, although she did notice some women together in groups of two or three. The women were all dressed in outfits similar to the one she was wearing, although the colors were different. Some of the blouses were halter tops and some of the skirts were much shorter. There were some women who looked like they were probably human, although she was having more and more trouble focusing on her surroundings. Fatigue was weighing down her body more with each step.

The cars formed a train that was pointed toward the gateway of a portal. Noting each side of the room had a portal, she assumed one was for coming and one for going. Looking at the portal the train was facing, she noticed it was smaller than the one back at the pactbuilding, but the eerie darkness was the same.

"Train ride to oblivion," she muttered to herself. "Great, just what I wanted, another portal to travel." Already exhausted, she wasn't looking forward to another trip through that blackness. As they entered the *shimvehi* and took their seats on a bench-like area, she found herself slumping.

Feeling her weight sagging against him, Liken put his arm around her and drew her close to his chest. "*Sherree*, you are crashing. Your body is adjusting to this planet's gravity and atmosphere. Your first trip through the interplanetary portal adds more stress. This portal merely takes us to a different city. Do not worry. Just relax. We will be home soon. You will sleep many hours. It is to be expected."

Before he finished the last word, he saw that she was sound asleep. Feeling her soft weight against him, he sighed. Finally, she was here.

Touching her hair with a soothing motion, he felt the *shimvehi* start to move. As his mind filled with images of the pleasures they would bring each other, he smiled.

Seduction had never promised to be so sweet.

Chapter Four

Where the hell was she?

Sharon looked at her surroundings and found nothing familiar. This wasn't her bed. This wasn't even her bedroom. Coming fully awake, she assessed the situation. She was lying in some sort of bed, although it was huge. The covers were quite soft but she couldn't place the material. It had the comfortable feel of cotton, but felt soft as silk. The walls were a light blue color. There were no windows and no doorway.

Was this a prison? If so, it was a comfortable one. There were pictures of strangely alien, but beautiful landscapes on three of the walls…

Alien.

With that thought, the events of the previous day came back to her. Startled, she sat up. Realizing she was stark naked, she immediately yanked the covers up around her. Oh, boy. Today was the first day of the rest of this farce.

Feeling energized, she looked around for some kind of clothing to put on. Her clothes had better be close by. As the wall slid open and Liken walked through, she had the mortifying realization that he must have undressed her. Oath or no oath, she didn't appreciate it.

Liken entered the room to discover Sharon sitting up in bed, bedclothes barely covering that naked body, cheeks rosy, eyes shining with outrage. In an instant, he was hard. He wanted to climb onto the bed and make her beg. Voice gruff, he asked, "How are you feeling, *sherree*?"

It was hard to be angry and maintain your dignity while stark naked under the thin cover of bedsheets. "Fine. Where are my clothes?"

"You will find garments in there," he replied with cautious gravity, although his amusement leaked through. She was shy, but he would change that inhibition. If he had his way, she would spend the rest of her knowing period naked and eager for him.

Sharon noticed the large bulge in the front of his pants. She knew if she didn't hurry, he would be joining her on the bed. Following his pointed finger, she saw a button off to the right. She assumed it opened a closet. "I'll meet you in a minute after I'm dressed." Her stomach growled.

Liken could hear the soft noise from the doorway. He smiled. "We will eat and then I will show you our home." He headed back out of the room. At the last second, he paused and turned back to her. "Regardless of what you choose to wear, *sherree*, you could not look more beautiful than at this moment." With that, he walked away and the wall slid shut behind him.

He was charming; she'd give him that. Smooth. She had the feeling that the charm was only one layer, though. Underneath it, she sensed a hard resolve. His desire was obvious and barely held in check. He would try to get something by charm, but if charm didn't work? She shivered a little at the thought.

Carefully crossing the room with a sheet wrapped around her, she pushed the button on the wall and watched as it slid open. It was a closet, just as she had thought.

She examined the clothes hanging there. There were numerous blouses and skirts. All were quite beautiful. They were made of a thin, silky material in different hues of colors. Some colors were like nothing she had seen on Earth. Blues and greens were more vibrant. The silver was especially lovely. There were even tiny panties with string ties. Looking everywhere, she couldn't find any bras. Just great. That silky material was going to outline everything.

Resigned, she selected a blouse and skirt of shimmering silver with tiny panties of the same color. There were strappy sandals to match. Putting everything on, she looked down at herself. The thin fabric of the blouse outlined the thrust of her nipples. The skirt was loose but hit just above the knee. Reluctantly, she wandered out into the hall.

Seeing a button on her right in the hall, she pushed it to reveal what was obviously a bathroom. It had a recognizable toilet, which she used gratefully. Seeing a stall to the side, she opened that door and discovered a shower with one handle. Feeling grubby, she decided to give it a shot. Removing her clothes and shoes, she set them on the floor and then turned the knob.

She was expecting water. She gave a little yelp of surprise as bright red liquid flooded from the nozzle high up on the wall. She reached out with one cautious hand and touched it. The temperature was hot, but not overly so. It felt more slippery than water, a little heavier. Weighing her grubbiness against the unknown, she decided to try it.

Stepping under the pouring liquid, she was surprised to discover it was like quicksilver. She hoped she didn't get dyed lobster red. The liquid poured over her skin, but when she stepped out, she was nearly dry. Grateful her skin hadn't turned the same hideous color, she put her clothes back on. Walking out into the hall, she kept going until she spotted open archways to the right and left. She could hear movement in the room to the right and turned toward it.

Entering the kitchen, she was surprised at the similarities to Earth kitchens. There was a long counter running along one side of the room. There were cabinets above it, although they had buttons she assumed would open each one. One wall was completely bare except for what looked like a small computer panel. It had a lot of buttons that presumably opened the wall or provided food transport maybe.

There was a mural carving of some kind on one wall that showed a waterfall. It was quite beautiful. In the center of the room, was a square table with four chairs. They could have come from any Earth kitchen. She was surprised to see that the table was already set. There were two settings, one on each side of the table. She saw plates and cups along with napkins, but no eating utensils.

In the center of the table sat a couple of bowls filled with oddly shaped fruits or vegetables, she guessed. There were some oblong dark green things, small orange shiny things that looked like berries, some larger purple things that were lumpy-looking, and even some bright yellow things that were almost square. She figured her first experience of exotic cuisine was about to start. Oh joy.

Liken set the last bowl onto the table and turned to smile at her. "Please do not assume I can cook. I am a guardian by profession. This is merely fruit." He moved and held out a chair for her to sit.

Pleased with his manners, she took it, watching as he sat down opposite her. "A guardian? What does that mean?"

Casually gathering an assortment from the various bowls, he began to put things on her plate. "A guardian is similar to your police officer. What do you call them? Cops? We protect those in need and prevent loss of life and property," Liken responded easily. It was nice to know that she was curious about him and his work.

Staring at him, she could see it. He did look like a cop. He could be gentle, but that underlying ruthlessness was there, too. "So, are you going to work today?" she asked hopefully. She shifted uncomfortably as she saw his gaze wander over her in appreciation. This outfit was no protection. She wanted as much distance between him and her tiny panties as possible. He couldn't seduce her if he wasn't around.

Looking amused, he shook his head. "I would not get assigned during my knowing period. I do not report back until after we have pledged." Breaking open a light purple fruit, he handed her half.

Eyeing it skeptically, but willing, she took a small, cautious bite. The sweetness burst in her mouth and she smiled with pleasure. She relaxed and continued to sample the different fruits. Making a face at the sour taste of the yellow one, she made a note to avoid it in the future. Very casually she said, "Yeah, I guess they've taken care of my job, too. I'm a librarian. After the noncomp papers are filed, I'll probably have a ton of stuff to catch up on." She waited for his reaction.

He had been eating his way through the fruit on his plate while she spoke. He paused. His face was still amused, but reproving. "There will be no noncomp papers, *sherree*." Reaching across the table, he took her chin in his hands, gently. Using his thumb to wipe the juice from her lips, he brought it slowly to his mouth. "We are very compatible. You will understand this quite soon."

Feeling the trail of heat left behind by his thumb, she swallowed the piece of fruit. She watched as he licked the juice from his thumb with sensual pleasure.

Her appetite for the fruit died and she looked away. Visibly gathering her composure, she tried reason. "Look, it doesn't have anything to do with you, okay? I like Earth. I have friends. I don't want to be a planet away from them. I have a job, an apartment, and responsibilities. A life. Mine. I've heard about this place. I don't remember much, but I do know that there are no unattached females over twenty. It's very male-dominated. Very old-style warrior mentality. I'm too independent to suit you or this place. I need different things. Trust me." She didn't hear the unconscious plea that had crept into her voice.

Liken studied her face during her oh-so-reasonable speech. Her eyes were sincere. She honestly believed she could not be happy here. "Maybe I can change your mind about what you need, *sherree*. Maybe I should start now." Rising, he came around the table and squatted next to her.

In alarm, she moved back against the seat as far as she could. "I didn't mean... Don't start messing with me again, okay?"

He smiled and raised his hand to her cheek. "Give me your mouth, *sherree*."

She shook her head and pressed into the cushion behind her.

Grabbing her hand, he pulled her slowly from her seat. "It is time. Come with me." Tugging her along behind him, he kept going until they reached the hallway and passed through the other archway into a living area. There were chairs and a couch along with a lot of buttons on the walls.

Gesturing her toward the long cushioned furniture, he went to a square structure coming out of one wall. Pulling out a drawer, he walked back across the room and handed her a small hand-held device, like a personal computer. It had a small screen at the top.

She moved closer to one side as he sat down beside her. "What's this?" She felt crowded by the weight and heat of his big body beside her. Even the big couch seemed too small for the two of them. She was overwhelmingly aware of him.

His eyes danced as she shifted further away from him, but he answered her seriously. "The Pactmaker has supplied your records to me. It is only fair that I do the same. These are my medical tests. I am completely healthy. I have been given my suppression shot this month, so pregnancy should not be a concern for you either. There are payment records from my employer, too, showing my ability to provide. There are statements from friends and family detailing my character. These are all records to let you know you are safe with me. That I am, what do humans usually say? A good guy."

"A prospective mate resume," she muttered. She knew the Pactmakers checked out everyone. Barely looking at the device, she put it aside. "Okay, I understand. You're wonderful. I'm sure you're kind to small kids and animals. But that doesn't mean I'm ready to just jump into bed with you. All these people know you, but I don't know you."

"You will." Moving the device from her side to the floor, he scooted over and leaned toward her. His eyes, those bright blue piercing eyes, were suddenly burning. "You chose Seduction. That means you will follow the rules of courtship according to that choice. We need to understand one another, *sherree*. Yesterday we kissed, mouth-to-mouth, tongue-to-tongue. Today we will do more of that. But today, you will allow me to run my hands over your body, to learn each curve. I will not remove your clothing."

His voice, which had turned husky, became firmer and more determined. "But, *sherree*, hear me well. I will do my best to take things as far as possible. I want you. I want to rock inside you and feel your sweet walls gripping me. I want to taste every inch of you, know what makes you tremble, what makes you wet."

A shiver went through Sharon followed by a wave of heat. He was seducing her with words, with mental images. It was brutal in its effectiveness. Licking her suddenly dry lips, she tried to form some response, but his gaze dropped to her lips and the words died in her throat. Her body was stiff with tension.

Reaching out one hand, he began running it along the edge of her blouse. Goosebumps followed in the wake of his fingers. His mouth was close to her ear as he said, "This garment is so thin. Already your breasts swell and your nipples harden. They ache for my touch, don't they? For my hands. For my mouth."

The moist warmth of his breath teased her ear as he leaned further down and began placing kisses along her throat. He continued kissing and talking as he worked his way down. "I would like to run my tongue around your nipples. I would play with them; make them ache for the sweet pressure of my mouth. Can you imagine how it will feel when I finally suck on them?" The mental picture of his mouth sucking on her breast nearly scalded her.

Kissing his way back up to her chin, his mouth moved to the corner of hers. As his hands moved from her neckline to the upper swells of her breasts, he whispered, "Easy…" She wasn't sure if he was talking to her or himself.

Sharon felt like she couldn't get enough air. His words and his touch were too much. She felt her chest rising and falling rapidly under his hands. She began to tremble as the excitement rushed through her. Already, she was growing wet, hot.

Running his tongue along her lips, he said, "Let me in."

Her trembling lips parted under firm pressure from his. The kiss was growing harder, hotter. Slanting his head, he took her deeper, thrusting along her tongue, running his tongue teasingly along her teeth and the inner edges of her lips. Then returning back inside, to stroke.

Her eyes closed and the muscles in her legs went lax. She began to duel with him, meeting each thrust with her own tongue, feeling the wet slide and unconsciously asking for more. With a moan, he gave her more.

Sharon felt one of his hands move down to her breast. He avoided the hard nipple, merely gripping lightly across the upper swell and then sliding around the side until he held her from underneath. As he began to shape her breast, kneading and pressing, she moaned and opened her mouth even wider. Their mouths met in a sexual feast.

She hardly noticed that her body had slipped downwards toward the arm of the couch. If she had looked down his body at that moment she might have seen the huge bulge of his aroused cock. But all she could feel or see was his mouth, his hands. She was drowning in a sea of sensation.

Lifting his mouth a fraction, he said softly, "I am going to touch those hard nipples now. You are aching for it, are you not?"

Sharon's answer was weak but understood. "Yes…"

Lifting his lips away from hers completely, he looked at her. Her mouth was swollen and wet. She opened her eyes. Those beautiful *mer* green eyes were dazed, the pupils dilated. Looking down, he saw the hard points of her nipples against the fabric. Bringing both his hands up, he covered her swollen breasts with them and felt those stiff nipples stabbing into his palms.

His cock, already hard, throbbed in time with his heartbeat. She was so responsive. He wanted to thrust inside her wet heat, to feel her close around his aching cock. He clung to his control.

Sharon gave a little cry as his hands finally covered her breasts. The contact of his palm against her nipples gave a little relief to her aching tips, but it was short lived. The ache continued to build. When he used his fingers and began playing with those twin points, she involuntarily arched her back, wanting more.

Twisting, lightly tugging, he played. Rough and gentle, by turns, his touch kept her surprised and restless. Looking into his face, she saw masculine satisfaction and hunger. For her. That look drew her almost as much as his touch.

As one of his hands began drifting downward onto her stomach, she felt that light brushing sensation in her mind again. Like the feel of his tongue lightly teasing her mouth before entrance, his mind touched hers, tempted. When she felt the brush again, she stiffened and said, "Wait!"

Lifting his hungry gaze to her again, he said, "No, *sherree*, I am within my rights." His hand continued over her stomach. Her legs tightened and she frantically drew them together in protest.

With a sigh, he placed a gentle kiss on her mouth. The hand and fingers at her breast never faltered, but the hand heading south paused. "Spread your legs for me now, Sharon. You have no choice in this. You chose yesterday when you took the Oath."

Her hands, hanging limply at her sides until now, came up in defense, grabbing the top of his. "I don't want this," she said desperately.

The hand under hers grabbed and then took her arms over her head. With one hand, he kept her pinned. She strained to get her hands free, but he was too strong. The hand at her breast began to move downward.

He said, a little less patiently, "That is a lie. Already your wetness shows through on the cloth. You made a vow, Sharon. Honor it or I will assume my vow to go in courtship stages is broken as well. Spread your legs for me," he demanded.

Sharon's heart was pounding in her ears. He was right. She did want him. She was throbbing, swollen and wet between her legs. She knew he meant what he said. Anger and passion were mixing inside her, making her arousal confusingly intense. She relaxed her legs, and with a look of resentment at his high-handedness, she slowly opened them.

His eyes were hard as they stared down into hers. "Wider."

She opened her legs wider and waited in trembling silence for his touch. When it finally came, she nearly arched off the couch. He ran his palm lightly over her mound. Just as he said, her wetness had soaked through the material making her feel as if it was skin on skin contact.

Looking into her eyes, he ran one finger along her lips, pausing briefly to tease her clitoris, then followed the line down to her opening. As that finger circled her opening, his thumb came back up to tease her clit with tiny strokes again and again. She arched up into his hand, but he merely continued the teasing pressure through the cloth.

She was burning up, wet and shaking. She'd felt passion before, but this kind of need was extreme and frightening. He seemed to know just where to touch and how. As he played and toyed with her, she grew wetter. The ache was intense. She needed more.

The slippery sounds of his fingers playing with her sweet sex pleased him. He made a little hum of approval in his throat. Her lower body was arched upwards in need. Her hips were unconsciously moving in an age-old rhythm against his hand. The temptation of her stiff nipples beckoned. Bending his head down, he found one hard nipple through the slippery material, took it into his mouth, and sucked.

Sharon heard a groaning sound and realized it had come from her. Her upper body arched, pressing her nipple even harder into the suction of his mouth. He pulled harder and then opened his mouth to lick around the aching tip. She was coming totally unglued. As he switched to the other nipple, laving it with his tongue and gently biting, then sucking, she whimpered and said, "Please..."

The fingers between her legs continued playing ruthlessly. She watched as he lifted his head from her aching breast, looking into her face. His eyes were heady-lidded, his mouth swollen and wet. He touched his tongue to the tip of her nipple and then said, "What do you want, *sherree*? Should I take this material from you and place my mouth on your breast? Or would you like me to touch you here..." one finger probed lightly inside her as far as the thin skirt and even thinner panties would allow, "with nothing to block me from giving you greater pleasure?"

Glancing down past his face to his body, she could see the hard outline of his arousal pressing against his pants. A tiny patch of wetness showed through the material near the top of his erection. Thinking about that hard bulge, she saw it flex against his pants. Just seeing it flex made her imagine his hard cock filling up that swollen, aching emptiness between her legs. She wanted that hard cock pressing inside her, filling her. She wanted him.

"It feels so good," she moaned as his hand continued to stroke. Her hands, still trapped in his large one, pushed against the pressure of his grip, but he held her still. Her very vulnerability excited them both.

The thumb against her clitoris pressed a little harder, then began circling the distended bud, sending bursts of pleasure outward with each touch. The tension in her body stretched tighter. His eyes continued to stare into hers as he watched her climb. "It can feel even better, *sherree*. Give in to it. Give in to me. Let go for me now."

Her hips were rising and falling against the pressure of his hand. She was on the edge, nearly desperate, half-blind with need. She felt her lower body tensing and tightening.

"Come for me, *sherree*. You are so wet. Give yourself to me." With those words, he pressed hard.

Sharon came apart under his hand. She closed her eyes as wave after wave of pleasure went through her. Caught in the grip of her climax, she couldn't do anything, think anything. There was only the pulsing pleasure of her body and the feel of his rough skin against her slick flesh through the cloth.

When she again became aware of herself, she could barely breathe from the overwhelming sensation of release. Her whole body was limp and flushed. She felt drained and shattered. Opening her eyes, she saw his face. He still looked intensely aroused, but mixed with the arousal was approval. He looked pleased.

Suddenly realizing just how wildly she'd been thrashing, how loudly she'd moaned, she felt shy. She tried to look away, but the hand between her legs came up to gently hold her face in place. The light musky scent of her arousal drifted to her from his fingers. She felt her face flush even more.

Liken smiled and placed a gentle kiss on her mouth. The hand holding her arms in place relaxed, and she brought her hands to her sides.

Liken's hungry gaze burned into her. He cleared his throat, his voice emerging husky and deep. "That was so beautiful, *sherree*. You are so beautiful."

She brought her hands to his chest and began scooting a little away from him. Now that her head was clearing, she suddenly wondered if he would push her further. She wanted him, but was afraid he would assume she'd fall in with *all* of his plans if she went further.

She also felt shaky and overwhelmed. She had never experienced anything like what had just occurred. The vulnerability was frightening. She had been pretty out of control. He had made her that way. Suddenly, she just wanted to get away from him for a while. She wanted to feel back in control. Would he let her go?

Liken knew she wasn't ready for a complete merging. As much as his throbbing cock would have liked her to be, she wasn't ready to continue. Her climax had nearly sent him over, too. He was too close to the edge and she was too inexperienced to proceed.

Sharon held her breath as he seemed to make up his mind. She knew if he truly pressed her, she was too vulnerable to say no. They both knew it.

Bringing his fingers from the side of her face, he brought them to his mouth. He ran his tongue along them slowly, watching her face, savoring the taste of her. Her heart seemed to stop.

He stood up from the couch as if in pain, and slowly moved away from her. A few steps away, he paused and quietly said, "You taste like my happiness." He stared at her a moment longer in silent hunger, then turned and slowly made his way out of the room.

Sharon felt her heart resume beating. Lying on the couch, still reeling, she could only wonder. He made her vulnerable. She had lost control, yet he had been able to walk away. Maybe he cared enough about her to leave unsatisfied. Or maybe he wasn't as vulnerable to her as she was to him. She didn't know.

She only knew that when she left this place, she would want him for the rest of her life. Her body was aching for his touch. Her emotions weren't too far behind. She didn't see a lot of happy endings ahead. Somebody was going to get hurt.

Sitting up and glancing toward the empty doorway she whispered sadly, "That's funny. You taste like heartache to me."

Chapter Five

Sharon retreated to her bedroom and a change of clothes. She wanted to explore the house, but the need to avoid Liken overrode her curiosity. She would be here for weeks. Right now, she concentrated on getting herself together.

From his point of view, she was sure it seemed simple. He could have sex with her for the next three weeks. At the end of that time, he could go to Earth, get pledged to her, then come back home. The next day, he could go to work just as he had before she'd entered his life. He wouldn't be leaving his home, his friends, and his job.

If he could stay on Earth, she might consider pledging with him. She knew it wasn't possible, though. Shimerian men visited Earth frequently, but couldn't remain more than three weeks at a time. Their bodies couldn't adjust. If they remained longer, they began to grow ill. Within a week after the onset of illness, they risked death if they didn't return to their own atmosphere. A lot of them came to Earth for a vacation, but no one stayed.

Another problem was their dominating ways and old world attitudes. Shimerian males were fiercely competitive. Given the lack of females, it was understandable. They were extremely dominant, too. Even Liken, who seemed gentle and patient a lot of the time, seemed to think subduing her sexually was the answer to any challenge from her. It might be exciting, but it was annoying, too. He was bigger and stronger, more sexually experienced. Any physical altercation could have only one result. She was too vulnerable to his attractions to think otherwise.

The thing that bothered her the most was the Shimerian viewpoint on love. To Shimerian males, love was not an important issue. Pledge relationships were based on sexual compatibility and mutual respect, even friendship.

She knew that she couldn't stay with Liken without falling in love with him. She couldn't be intimate with him day after day, living with him, talking to him, without falling for him along the way. That knowledge deep inside herself was one of the reasons he scared her so badly.

If she could just accept what was happening as a good time, "interplanetary nookie" as she had joked with Kate, then it might be different. But something inside her responded to him emotionally.

She didn't like it. She had been right when she'd laid eyes on him. He was a heartbreaker. Sitting on the bed, lost in her thoughts, she almost didn't hear him when the door slid open and he stuck his head in the doorway.

"Sharon, we are due to meet with my brother for midmeal. Are you ready to go?" He took in the turmoil on her face and wisely kept his tone neutral.

She could sit on the bed all day brooding, but it wasn't going to solve anything. She stood up and walked toward him. "Sure," she sighed. "Let's go." Following on his heels, she trailed behind him through the house and out the sliding front door. When they got outside, she stopped in wonder.

"It's beautiful here," she said in surprise as her surroundings struck her. She had been asleep the night before when he brought her in. Looking around, she saw a row of dwellings, side by side in the pink glow of the day. Again, the bricklike material was glowing like the office buildings had been the night before. Most were box-like in shape, without windows.

However, the facades of the dwellings had wonderful carvings decorating them. They depicted landscapes of lush vegetation. The glow seemed to make them more alive, more beautiful.

Most of the dwellings had plants growing around the buildings. The large leaves were a light yellow, but with flowers of red and delicate pink. There were black walkways leading to the entrance of each building. She would have expected grass yards around the walkways, but instead there was a lush carpeting of some blanketing foliage. It had tiny pink flowers in contrast to the creamy white of the dense leaves. It was strange, but also strangely beautiful.

Liken smiled, pleased with her appreciation of his home. "Thank you, *sherree*. It is like this always. The temperature rarely varies. We do not have the seasons here as you have on Earth."

He began to walk with her along the black central walkway between the two rows of dwellings. He took her hand in his, but she pulled it back after only a few seconds and pointed out a nearby plant. He did not reach for her hand again. As they walked, she asked questions about the different plants and dwelling carvings. He answered her questions easily, although he did shrug with laughing ignorance when she asked for the names of some of the flowers.

They passed several couples strolling hand in hand, most of them Shimerian males with Earth females. The couples were distantly friendly, calling out greetings as they passed. She could tell that they knew Liken and by their admiring glances could tell that he was well liked. He avoided lengthy introductions by keeping them moving, responding in a friendly manner that didn't encourage further conversation.

When they were alone again, she continued to pepper him with eager questions. As they talked, she lost some of her guardedness and began to relax with him. When Liken casually took her hand in his this time, she merely smiled and kept talking.

He was surprised at the simple pleasure he took in her company. Her enthusiasm and curiosity were a delight. She had a bright, inquisitive mind. As he answered her questions, he found himself charmed.

Sharon had a sudden thought. "Where are we going? I mean, I know you said lunch with your brother, but are we eating at his house? Does he live near here?" Tilting her head up at him, her hand still trustingly in his, she asked, "Do we have to go through a portal?" Her enthusiasm waned a little. She wasn't eager to travel through another portal.

He shook his head. "This city is called Glowen'da. We live close to the city center. There is a public eatery there where we will meet my brother. He lives in Karten'sha. It is a quick trip through the western portal. Knowing your love for portals, I asked him to meet us here today." His gaze was teasing.

She smiled in relief. "I know portals are commonplace here, but I'd like to get used to them gradually if you don't mind. Walking into that blackness feels like stepping off a cliff and hoping there's something to catch you below. You probably don't think twice about it anymore, but it's a little eerie to me."

Tugging her hand, he pulled her close and gave her a hug. "I know there is a lot of change for you, *sherree*. Just remember that I am here at your side." Giving her one last squeeze, he released her and pointed toward a group of buildings a couple of blocks away. "There is the eatery. It is called *Jerlanks*."

The building looked much like the surrounding office buildings. Much larger than private dwellings, each building had a carving on the outside that effectively demonstrated its function. *Jerlanks* had a large carving of people eating and drinking, some heads tossed back with laughter, like a large party was occurring within its walls.

Walking faster now, they reached the building in very little time. As they entered through the archway, Sharon saw a large dining area filled with square tables. Looking around the room, she was struck by the large number of males present. There were about ten women, all with male companions. The women were all wearing thin outfits similar to hers. The rest of the tables, maybe twenty-five or thirty, were crowded three or four to a table with men.

As she and Liken paused to scan the room, a noticeable hush descended. Feeling as if every eye in the room was on them, she hoped Liken located his brother fast. She was extremely conscious of male eyes lingering on the prominent thrust of her nipples beneath the blouse. As a man stood at one of the back tables and motioned to them, she followed Liken in relief. Conversation again resumed around them as they threaded their way through the tables.

Approaching Liken's brother, she noticed immediately that he was the good-looking guy who had given Kate a hard time. Liken nodded his head at the man. He smiled even as his voice comfortably teased, "Sharon, my brother, Tair. Do not let him charm you." His voice filled with pride as he introduced them more formally. "Tair, this is my pactmate, Sharon." Gesturing toward Tair, he said, "*Sherree*, you remember Tair. He was present at our Oath ceremony."

It was easy to believe they were brothers. Both had the same powerful build, although Tair was a little leaner. His dark hair was longer than Liken's hair, with more curl to it. The arrogant stance and charisma were identical, though. Duel heartbreakers, she decided. She gave him the beginnings of a shy smile.

Smiling warmly in response, Tair took her hand in his and said, "Welcome, Sharon. It is a pleasure to meet my future link. Liken doesn't deserve you, but he was ever lucky."

Sharon smiled back helplessly. She had no idea what he meant by link, but he really was charming. "It's nice to meet you, too. Although you're really jumping the gun since we only took the oath yesterday." She added quickly, "We still have three weeks to decide if we're compatible."

Tair arched a questioning eyebrow in Liken's direction at her comment, and a silent message passed between the two men. "Ahhh. My apologies. Apparently my brother has not worked his magic on you yet." His eyes were amused.

When Liken lightly hit his arm, the amusement only grew. "Please sit with me." With an easy gallantry that reminded her of Liken, Tair pulled out a chair and motioned for her to sit.

Taking a seat to his left as he gestured, she saw Liken sit down in one beside her. They were each sitting on one side of the square table. She felt dwarfed between the two men.

Looking over at Tair, she said quite innocently, "You must be the one with magic. I don't think I've ever seen anyone leave Kate speechless before. She's used to getting her way. I was impressed at the oath yesterday."

Tair laughed. "Well, I can believe she would be a worthy challenge to any opponent at any game. She was quite fierce in her protection of you."

Suddenly swamped with missing her friend, Sharon's smile dimmed. "Yes, she is. She's a very loyal friend." Images of the good and bad times she had shared with Kate flashed through her mind. She wished fiercely that she could see her friend and tell her what had happened so far.

Sensing her longing, Tair placed his hand over hers. He sought to reassure her, although he couldn't quite contain a secretive smile at the knowledge that the two friends would be together sooner than either of them could imagine. "Sharon, you will always have her friendship. You will be together with her again. You have my oath."

Shrugging off her sudden mood, she attempted to lighten the tone of the conversation. With a brisk nod of her head, she said, "Of course. It's only three weeks. I'm just used to having her around to try to arrange my life. Kate has very definite ideas on making your own happiness."

Her smile widening into a grin, she said, "she just happens to think she knows the best way for everyone to go about it." Her grin slowly turned into a chuckle.

Tair's eyes were dark with appreciation. "Yes, I believe she does. That confidence is very apparent. I doubt she gets surprised very often."

Sharon laughed. "The horrible part is she's usually right. Of course, it was her bright idea that got me into this, uh...situation...in the first place." The memory of a much younger Kate urging her to sign passed through her mind. With a shake of her head at their youthful naiveté, she glanced toward Liken.

Liken was smiling. "So I have Kate to thank for my good fortune. For that I owe her much. Perhaps she will be rewarded in the future for her good deed." He shot a sidelong glance at Tair.

Tair's eyes held a promise. "I have no doubt she will."

At that moment a man appeared, asking if they were ready to state their selections. Sharon gave Liken a questioning look. He said to her, "If it pleases you, I will select for you. I know you are not yet familiar with the foods here."

He was certainly being careful about appearing domineering. Giving an assenting nod, Sharon listened as he ordered. Nothing was familiar, but she hoped for the best.

After the waiter disappeared, Liken turned to Sharon. "Forgive me, *sherree*, but I need to ask Tair about something."

He turned to Tair. "What is happening with Bek?"

As Tair filled him in, Sharon realized they were discussing one of his work cases. Tair must be a cop, too, from the way he talked. As the waiter brought them their food, conversation around the table turned to lighter topics.

Tair asked how she had enjoyed her time on Shimeria thus far. Fighting off a vivid memory of their activities on the couch that morning, Sharon felt her cheeks warm. Her enthusiastic response to his caresses still mortified her. Making a polite response, she avoided Liken's knowing gaze.

Quickly, Sharon began complimenting the food. As they told her the name of each dish, she asked questions and spoke enthusiastically of the beauty of the neighborhood. Both men made an effort to keep her entertained and at ease. Many times, masculine heads turned at the sound of her laughter during the meal.

Lunch passed quickly. Tair finally said regretfully, "I have enjoyed this time much, but I cannot stay longer. I must report back to my command." His signaling nod brought the waiter immediately. The waiter took his ID card and disappeared into the other room. Coming back almost immediately, he handed the card back to Tair with polite thanks. Tair stood and gave a little bow toward the two of them. "Please stay and enjoy. I have paid for all of us."

Liken made a noise of protest, but Tair overruled him. "It is my right as link of the oath couple." Offering a slap to Liken's shoulder, he said, "Guard her well, brother. Else some sneaky male might steal this delight." With a wink at Sharon, he left.

Liken's smile was rueful as he heard Sharon laugh. "Charm in abundance, I know. Should I worry he has swayed you with his tricks?" His eyes were teasing.

"Maybe. He's pretty smooth." Her smile was flirtatious. "Not jealous of big brother, are you?" she asked with false innocence.

He shook his head. "He might make you laugh, *sherree*, but you are mine in the end. Besides, that surface charm covers steel. He can be very ruthless. He took great pains to set you at ease. I appreciated it. I trust my brother."

His eyes took on a hard gleam as they swept the restaurant. His voice matched his eyes as he said quietly, "I am not so tolerant of others." At his look and words, several of the men who had been eyeing Sharon quickly turned away.

Sharon was surprised to hear the conversation around her dip and then pick up volume again. Then she remembered the Shimerian hearing. A little part of her perked up at his jealousy. He was publicly stating his claim. His heart might not be vulnerable, but he was feeling possessive. It was a start. If he could feel jealousy, those feelings could deepen over time. Love might be possible.

Feeling a little lighter, she asked, "What do we do now?" Almost immediately she realized she would probably get some embarrassing answer.

Although his eyes gleamed, he merely said courteously, "I thought I would show you the city. "

She nodded her assent eagerly. Going back to the house would put them in intimate territory. She wasn't ready to tangle with him again.

Of course, she knew that she couldn't put it off indefinitely.

Chapter Six

They explored Glowen'da for the rest of the day. As they walked around the city, Sharon realized the similarities to Earth. The contact and constant flow of travelers between the two planets were slowly blending the cultures. Although the landscape was alien, there was a familiarity she felt as she walked and asked questions.

She was surprised as well by how much she and Liken had in common. They had both lost their parents at a young age. They both enjoyed reading and similar types of music. As they went from place to place, there was a strange sense of comfort between them. Liken surprised her with his enthusiasm. He seemed to be having a good time just being with her, seeing things through her eyes. It was flattering.

Inevitably, after a time, Liken turned them toward home. Sharon's feet and legs were beginning to feel the effects of an afternoon spent walking. When they reached the house, she felt her earlier tension begin to return. Turning quickly toward the bedroom, she said, "I'll just rest a while."

Liken stopped her with a hand on her arm. "You can rest in here, *sherree*."

She looked away from him. Her gaze alighted on the couch and she immediately took a step back. "I don't think so." Their conversation after the Oath ceremony, when he said he could repeat any intimacy, flashed through her head.

Pulling her into his arms, he said, "I had hoped we made progress this afternoon. Why do you still fear me?"

She looked into his face. He seemed honestly perplexed. "I'm not afraid of you. I just think we should take things slowly, that's all." In fact, she was hoping they could put off any form of intimacy for several days...or more. She needed time.

A dawning understanding passed over his face. "I think I see. You do not fear me. You fear yourself."

"Don't be ridiculous." She felt the first stirrings of anger.

"Very well, then. You fear your response to me." He sounded understanding, but his face was hardening. He was growing frustrated with her.

Sharon said, "I don't want to fight. I just want you to leave me alone for awhile." It was time to put more distance between them, if she could.

"This I will not do." His voice was firm. "You are trying to retreat. You hide from me but more...you hide from yourself. You want me just as much as I want you. You are bound to honor your oath. This is our knowing period. What we do is expected."

"I didn't expect it, okay? " Her voice was rising. "I'm tired of you throwing duty in my face. I know what I vowed. Theoretically, I guess, just skipping off planet and having sex with a strange alien guy is supposed to be easy. But it's not. I'm not casual. The two guys I was with before may not have been heroes, but they were decent guys that I cared about. You want me to just get naked and have sex with you like it's easy. It's not. I've never been with someone like you. You make me feel..." her voice faltered. Sharon suddenly realized that she was afraid of how he made her feel.

"Out of control? Hot? Overwhelmed?" he suggested huskily.

Sharon paused at his words, and thinking quickly, nodded. "Okay fine. All of those things." She didn't like where this discussion was going.

"Is that so bad, *sherree*? The attraction between us is intense. It is our fortune. You say you do not like feeling out of control, but I know sexually, it makes you hot. I know seeing you that way makes me hot. You may not be comfortable and safe like in your controlled world, but you like what I say to you. You like what I do to you. I would wager that right now you are wet from my words. Perhaps you need to learn that there is no harm in giving up control. That you are safe with me."

He was right, but she didn't like admitting it. She was wet from his words. She blushed, knowing her tightened nipples were obvious against the thin barrier of her top. There was no way he could fail to notice her obvious arousal. Her body was betraying her.

Liken could see and sense how affected she was by his words and presence. He reached out and ran his hands along the sides of her body in one slow stroke. Sharon tried to move away, but he merely picked her up and carried her to the couch. Coming down on top of her, he again pinioned her hands as he had earlier.

Peering into her face, his voice brooked no argument. "I will not take you tonight. I will bring you to peak with my hands and my mouth on this couch until we grow hungry. We will eat the evemeal with you in my lap, my hands on your body. Then we will return to this couch. You will come for me, *sherree*. You will ache and come and ache for more."

She swallowed roughly.

"You will get used to this hunger between us. Your comfort with me will be assured. But know this, tomorrow there will be no clothing between us. You will not hide behind the safety of your inhibitions. I am a Shimerian male. We are highly sexual, dominant beings. I will not pretend otherwise. To truly know me, you must be willing to know yourself."

Somewhat angrily, his mouth came down on hers.

His hard kiss gradually gentled into teasing caresses. As she responded with less reluctance and more enthusiasm, he left no part of her untouched. The feel of his hands and mouth through the thin barrier of her clothes was overwhelming.

The next hours were unbelievable. He was relentless. Using his hands and mouth, he brought her to climax after climax. As he had promised, he never removed her clothes. Even sitting at the table, eating, one hand always roamed her body. Leaning back against his chest, she accepted bites of food as she arched into the fingers tweaking her nipple or gliding between her legs.

Later, back on the couch, her body grew exhausted. When he finally sat up and moved away from her, she felt like there wasn't a nerve on her body that hadn't been stroked. She was swollen, her breasts tender. Between her legs, she throbbed and felt a pulsing awareness of him with every beat of her heart.

Looking into his harsh countenance, she marveled at his control. He hadn't lost it once. It was frightening. His face was lined with the costs of his effort, but he had certainly made his point.

Early on, her defenses had toppled. She had eagerly sought his caresses, even encouraged them. He had given her pleasure after pleasure, but always stopped short of removing her clothing. He had a deeply ingrained sense of honor. He hadn't misused her or gone back on his word.

She couldn't pretend to herself any longer. She did know a lot about this man. She did want him. She couldn't fight both him and herself any longer.

Getting up on shaky legs, she faced him. "I'm going to sleep now. You've made your point. I want you. I'm not really afraid of you." She felt vulnerable, exposed. "We'll sleep together tomorrow. But you might think about this: sex isn't enough to tie me to you permanently. I may go to my grave wanting you, but I'll be buried on Earth. I'm not going to get lost in you and your world. I'm entitled to my own dreams."

He looked genuinely shocked. "I don't want to take everything from you, Sharon. I want to build a life together with you. If a life on Earth was possible, I would be there with you."

She looked skeptical. "Easily said, when you'll never have to do it. It's so easy for you. You get everything you want." She gave him a level look and then left the room.

He watched as she left, his body screaming for release, his emotions in turmoil. Liken felt like howling. He dropped his head into his hands. The only thing he truly wanted was *her*.

In the quiet of the room he was temporarily using as a sleep chamber, the night progressed and the activity of the previous hours kept playing through his mind to torment him. He remembered her softness, her response to his caresses, and the way her body would get wet at his touch.

That night Liken got very little sleep. Besides the aching frustration of his body, his thoughts restlessly turned the situation with Sharon over and over. She was resentful of leaving her homeworld and her own plans. She felt fearful of her vulnerability to him. Perhaps the best way to lessen that fear was to demonstrate to her that she had power over him as well. That wouldn't be any problem.

He sighed. Only someone with her level of inexperience could have missed the effect she had on him. His cock felt painful with the need to go to her and show her immediately.

Another problem was her need for control, for not letting go. She didn't like to lose control, didn't like to be open and vulnerable. Well, she was fighting a losing battle. She was wrong in not realizing sex could form a level of intimacy more powerful than a hundred of her Earth "dates." She was so powerful in her vulnerability and so totally unaware of it.

She was so beautiful and honest in her responses. It reached him on an emotional level that he had never experienced with any previous partners. Because she was so reluctant to share herself, it merely made the sharing more poignant, more special.

He felt powerful when he drew a response from her, it was true. But at the same time, he felt helplessly drawn to her. He wanted her more than he had wanted any other woman physically. Mentally, he wanted to know her thoughts, to see the world from her viewpoint. Emotionally, he wanted to bring joy to her life and watch those eyes light from within with happiness. He was well and truly mired in her. There could be no going back at this point.

He turned onto his back and stared at the ceiling. He had to find a way to make her want to stay. With a grimace he faced his next thought. He had been very careful with her thus far. Once they began having sex, the urge to merge telepathically would grow stronger. He would eventually lose control.

If she worried about being lost in him now, he could imagine her reaction to that. She would be horrified and panic. If she rejected him during the merge, he could hurt her terribly. He had to initiate her carefully.

When they did merge, she could leave him at a later time. The loss of immediate mental intimacy would be incredibly painful for him. He was risking a lot more than she seemed to think. He had to find a way to bind her to him heart, mind, and soul.

He sighed. Easy for him, she had said. Right.

* * * * *

Sharon spent a restless night tossing and turning in her bed. She could hear Liken's movements in the other bedroom. The house was so quiet that she could hear the rustle of the sheets as he turned one way and then another. She tensed a couple of times as she heard him get up from the bed and pace the room.

She knew he could by rights come into her room and begin touching her again. Her body, exhausted and swollen, still ached with the knowledge of what he would do to her. Yet, each time, he returned to bed without entering her room. She was relieved. Mostly.

She thought about why he hadn't just finished things between them tonight. He wanted her to get used to him sexually. She couldn't help but wonder why he was being so careful. He could have pushed her into more. She was helpless in her attraction to him. There was more to his caution than he was telling her. She felt sure of it.

He was an alien. Granted, he appeared to have the same equipment as any Earth male. Why the caution? Wasn't sex the same? She thought about the two times she'd felt his mind brush against hers. She didn't like the thought that he might enter her mind the way he would enter her body. She had avoided asking him about the mind thing because it was too scary.

There had been too many things happening in too short a time. She felt overwhelmed. She hadn't wanted to deal with even one more surprise—especially the thought of him inside her head. Would he be able to read all her thoughts? Her secrets? Would he be able to do it anytime or just during sex? What could he do? She felt like running away from him as far and as fast as she could. Her heartbeat pounding in her ears, she struggled to calm down and reason things out.

Liken's sudden appearance in the doorway at that moment nearly scared her to death. She gave a muffled shriek and stared at him in alarm.

"Sharon, what is frightening you?" he asked gently as he came into the room and sat down on the edge of the bed. He was dressed only in a pair of loose black pants, tied at the top with a small white cord. His chest, large and muscular, gleamed in the dim light as the lights suddenly became a little brighter.

"Did you do that?" she asked in surprise.

"What?" he seemed confused by her question.

"The lights. How did you make them brighter? Where are they?" She kept looking around the room for some kind of light source.

He seemed to be choosing his words carefully. "Yes. I did make it brighter in here. I will show you how another time. You are very anxious. What is wrong?" His voice was soothing.

It was strange. Since he had entered the room, she had been feeling calmer. She didn't know if it was his presence or the interruption from her disturbing thoughts. She needed to get a grip. Whatever the mind thing was, she couldn't just freak out about it and have a heart attack. She needed to know more about it. Maybe it wasn't what she thought at all.

She needed to approach this logically and get more information. Liken reached out and gently brushed her hair off her forehead. Looking at his face etched with concern, she decided now was as good a time as any.

"Liken, what is that mind thing you do?" Her eyes bravely held his as she braced for the worst.

His face carefully went blank. "This is what has you so fearful?" He had hoped to avoid the explanation until after their merge.

"Well, yes. I mean, I started thinking about tomorrow. About us being together..." her voice grew a little fainter. "What's going to happen? Will you be inside me? Inside my head?"

Liken could see even in the dim light her cheeks were flushed. She was embarrassed, but still wanting answers. He felt an unexpected wave of tenderness go through him. How to explain without scaring her to death? "*Sherree*, you don't have to be fearful. When our bodies join, our minds will join as well. It is a wonderful thing, a beautiful thing."

She sat up a little, carefully keeping the sheet around her. "Okay, but what does that mean? Is it just for a moment? I mean, am I going to have you in my head all the time after that?"

She looked very unhappy at the thought. "Not exactly. It's a little hard to explain. I would rather show you than try to describe it." He was aroused at the mere idea of it. He was trying to hide his growing arousal from her, but it was impossible to hide the hardness pressing outward from his pants.

Pinned by his heavy-lidded gaze, Sharon felt uneasy. He wasn't really answering her. "What's the big secret? Why won't you tell me?"

Liken didn't want to lie to her, but he couldn't tell her either. For a fleeting second he wished she had picked Challenge or Capture. He could have merged with her immediately without her consent. It would have been shocking and painful for her, but effective.

The impulse to possess her was strong and the talk of merging was making him hot. Reminding himself that Sharon would not be Sharon if she had picked one of the other options, he decided to give her a small preview without revealing everything. It might lesson her fear. Provided he could stay in control enough to withdraw in time. *Time...*

Suddenly he realized it was past halfeve. In fact, his time restriction was up. He could take her now. Looking into her face he realized she was growing angry at his evasion. She had no idea that they could now move to the last stage. Perhaps that could work to his advantage.

He moved his body closer to hers on the bed. Something must have shown in his face because Sharon suddenly gave a violent pull on her sheets. It sent him tumbling to the floor.

He ended up sprawled on his butt, eyes wide in shock. It was a contest as to which of them was more surprised. Her hand flew to her mouth and her eyes were huge.

Jumping out of bed, she was careful to wrap the sheet around her body quickly. Backing toward the door, she let out a nervous little giggle before she could stop herself. "I really didn't mean to do that. It's just...you had that look you get right before you pounce on me. I was just going to grab the sheet and get out of bed..." Her voice was shaky with suppressed laughter.

"You think thrusting me to the floor is funny, do you?" His voice was fierce, but she could see a gleam of amusement in his eyes. He stood up with fluid grace and began stalking toward her slowly.

"No, not really." She tried not to laugh, but he had looked so shocked. It was the first time she had ever had him at a disadvantage and it felt good. "I can't help it if you're clumsy, you know…" She continued to back down the hallway. Looking around wildly, she turned around quickly and made a sudden break for the kitchen.

Giving a mock growl, he caught her quickly and swung her into his arms. Laughing, he managed to keep hold of her while she wiggled and squirmed. Looking into her laughing eyes and flushed face, he had never wanted her more. His expression changed to open desire.

Sharon stopped squirming as she instantly became aware of her position. Looking down, she realized the sheet had become loosened and was dangerously close to falling off. With a quick grab, she managed to keep from losing it altogether. Clutching it to her, she looked up into his face.

In his eyes was a naked hunger that took her breath away. Swallowing past the sudden lump in her throat, she said, "I think you should put me down now."

His arms tightened. Suddenly moving toward her bedroom, he agreed. "Yes, I think I should."

When he reached the bed, he gently put her down on her back, and then followed her. Covering her body with his own, he kept most of his weight on his elbows as he gazed into her face.

Sharon began to tremble. "It's time, isn't it? We're not going to stop this time." Her eyes searched his face, although she already knew the answer.

Shifting his weight to one side, his body no longer looming over her, he moved the other arm across her until his hand gently closed on hers. Her fingers were white where they gripped the sheet. "No, *sherree*. We're not going to stop this time…" His voice was husky with need.

He began prying her fingers from the death grip on the sheet. Unconsciously responding to the need in his tone, she began to relax her grip. When she let go, he took her hand and slowly brought it to his mouth. Gently kissing her fingers, his mouth moved to the palm of her hand. She felt the moist heat of his mouth on the sensitive center of her hand as he gently licked then sucked. She felt a wave of heat all the way to her toes. Her trembling increased.

Feeling her body tremble, he released her hand and began gently stroking her hair. "*Sherree*, I know you are afraid of the merging." He hesitated. "We will go slowly. We will do this thing together." Again, he searched for words. "I have not merged before either. I know what I have been told. But that is not the same as doing it. My mind will touch yours, just as my body touches yours. I will go slowly, but there will come a point when I lose control. You will feel but a brief pain, a flash, like a piercing headache. And then there will be only pleasure for both of us."

He waited for her response. The ache to possess her was like a living thing inside him.

She raised a trembling hand to his face. "Okay." Her eyes were tear-bright as she put a shaky smile on her face. "We'll try this together. I can handle a little headache."

At the gentle touch of her hand on his face, he shuddered. He was so proud of her he could barely breathe. "*Sherree*, I need you to trust me in this. When the time comes, I am asking you not to turn away or fight me. It will be frightening, but please trust that it will be all right in the end. I will not let anything bad happen to you. You know that, do you not?" The promise in his voice eased her as nothing else could.

Her eyes were full of dawning wonder. "I do know that." This big, fierce man was practically vibrating from her touch on his face. He wanted her very badly, but he was trying very hard to reassure her. He didn't just want her. He wanted her willing. He wanted her to trust him.

This wasn't just sex. Until this moment, she had felt completely helpless in her attraction to him. Now, she suddenly understood that he was just as helpless in his attraction to her. It was quite a revelation. Somehow, it made her feel stronger, more powerful. She had felt off balance and overwhelmed since he had suddenly appeared. Now, for the first time since that moment, she understood that maybe he had felt just as off balance.

She had been trying to cope with sudden changes, but he had been trying to figure out how to make that coping easier for her. She still felt nervous, but a lot of her fear vanished. He was doing the best that he could, just as she was. Moving her hand from his face to behind his head, she began to pull him toward her. When she felt his breath on her mouth, she whispered, "I trust you, Liken."

With a little moan, he took her mouth. The kiss was fierce, his mouth hard and demanding. Thrusting his tongue between her lips, he swept inside, enjoying the sweet taste of her. When her tongue began to duel with his, his control, already sketchy, slipped. He moved his hand from her hair and swept it to the edge of the sheet to pull it down. Hearing her low gasp, he suddenly paused and pulled back. "I am sorry, *sherree*." His breath was coming in pants. "I want you so much..." With effort, he pulled himself back under control.

Her lips were swollen and she looked dazed. With more tenderness, he returned to her mouth and began gentle, biting little kisses. He moved his mouth across her face to her ear, and then slowly down the side of her neck. His hand, at the top of the sheet, began to inch it down. When at last it was down to her waist, he pulled back a little to look at her.

Sharon opened her eyes. He had stopped the drugging kisses to the side of her neck. She froze as she realized the sheet was now down by her waist. His face was pulled tight, his eyes nearly black with wanting. His gaze moved over her breasts like a physical touch. She could feel her nipples hardening almost painfully.

With a little sound of approval, he moved his head down and began to suck. With a loud moan, she arched into his mouth. Pulling back a little, he began running his tongue around and around the hardened nipple. "You are so beautiful...so responsive..."

He switched to the other breast and began licking and sucking it. "I want them hard and red from my mouth..." His hand moved back to her abandoned breast and began massaging. Sharon shuddered with the pleasure of it. "You feel so good to me, *sherree*..." His mouth continued to tease and torment her breast.

His fingers on the other breast began to focus on her nipple. He gently rolled and pulled. Sharon could not hold back another moan. He quickly switched breasts. Licking, sucking, even gently biting, his mouth was driving her out of her mind. She brought both hands to the back of his head and pressed him even closer.

With a pleased chuckle, he complied, growing rougher, more demanding. "That's it...you are feeling it now, are you not?" She was twisting underneath him, trying to get closer. "I think I will keep these nipples hard and wanting all the time. You are very sensitive. I plan to discover how sensitive..."

Her hips were rising and falling. He was still on his side, half bent over her. He caught the edge of the sheet in his hand as her hips rolled upward and pulled it quickly past her waist. Pulling back from her breast, he looked down at what he had revealed.

She was incredible. Those full breasts tapered to a small waist then rounded to generous hips. The dark triangle of hair between her long legs was glinting with moisture. He felt his mouth water.

With a little groan, he moved so that his upper body was between her legs. She raised up a little on her elbows to look down at him. Holding her gaze, he began placing light kisses on her stomach around her navel. She looked dazed, as if she was in a trance. The musky smell of her sex lured him downward. Still holding her gaze, he licked down her stomach to just above her curls. Her head went back and her entire body shuddered.

Placing light kisses into her curls, he kept his gaze on her face. Blowing gently into her soft hair, he said firmly, "Look at me." She lifted her head slowly as if it was heavily weighted. Green eyes locked with blue as he said, "Watch me taste you..."

With that, he swept his tongue in one long glide from her clitoris downward. Probing her opening, he pushed his tongue into her as far as it would go, and then journeyed back to circle her clit. He began to gently lap, reveling in her taste, her scent. He moaned low in his throat and the vibration nearly sent Sharon over the edge.

Her body had been reduced to sheer sensation. The feel of his hands as they massaged and tormented her breasts, the feel of his mouth and tongue between her legs, were all too much. She was hot, her body aching. She couldn't seem to get enough air. He was eating her alive.

She was wetter than she'd ever been in her life. She could feel that slick wetness dripping down. She could see his head moving between her legs. As he gently sucked on her clitoris, his demanding gaze held her captive. One hand moved from her breast. There was a sudden pressure inside her sex as one long finger probed. She felt herself tightening, the tension building. She wanted his hardness between her legs, filling her up. She wanted his cock plunging into her. She muttered, "Please..."

He moved back from her to stand up. Still lying on her elbows, she watched him as he untied the top of his pants and pulled them down, stepping out of them. He wore nothing underneath. He stood back up, already moving to get back on the bed.

"Wait!" At her word, he froze in surprise. Licking her lips without realizing just how provocative the sight was to Liken, she said huskily, "I want to see you."

With a visible nod in relief, he walked to the head of the bed. Turning her body toward him, she took a slow inventory. He was magnificent. The hard, sculpted muscles of his chest gave way to a narrow waist and lean hips.

His cock thrust upward proudly toward his stomach. It was larger than the ones she had seen before. Just the sight of it made her mouth go dry. It was about eight inches long, with a large tip already nearly purple in color. As she looked, it gave a little jump, as if in recognition. With a start, her gaze leapt up to his face. He was watching her reaction closely. With a little smile of approval, she licked her lips. "Wow. You are amazing."

A broad grin spread across his face. Apparently, human male or alien male, they all wanted some sign of approval when their masculinity was on the line. His voice was deep and rough. "I am glad you think so, *sherree.*"

Her smile widened in response. Reaching out her hand slowly, she let one fingertip glide from the tip of his cock all the way to the base. When she reached the base, she encircled it with the rest of her hand. He was so large; she could barely put her fingers around him. His answering groan was so loud, she nearly let him go.

With lightning reflexes, he brought his hand over hers, holding it in place. His head was thrown back with his eyes tightly shut in pleasure. Sharon felt her body tense with wanting. He looked so hot. As his hand moved hers on his cock in slow up and down motions she watched the planes of his face grow harsher.

He looked powerful and vulnerable at the same time. His masculine beauty singed her senses. Feeling a shudder move through him, she felt powerful. She suddenly stopped the motion of her hand. "Look at me," she demanded.

He opened his eyes abruptly. He looked wild, nearly out of control. She could see him visibly trying to grab hold of his discipline. Some devil within her wanted to push him right to the edge. To make him as out of control as he always made her.

Without warning, she leaned over and took as much of him into her mouth as she could. The feel of his hardness in her mouth was nearly indescribable. His skin was smooth and soft, although his cock was hard and huge in her mouth. She could actually feel him throb as she lightly stroked her tongue along his length.

Liken froze, every muscle in his body locking into place. He was totally focused on the moist heat of Sharon's mouth on his cock. It was unbelievable. Jerking his hand out from under hers, he brought both hands up to her head, trying to hold her in place. His knees felt weak and he could literally feel the blood drain from his face.

She disregarded his gesture and began to move her head up and down, her mouth moving almost the length of his cock, sucking. His heart seemed to stop in his chest. He could barely breath. His hands clenched fistfuls of her hair as she moved again and again carrying him closer to the edge. With a moan, he gave himself up to the pleasure and to her. He let her take him with her mouth until he knew he was in danger of coming.

Drawing on every ounce of discipline he possessed, he pulled her head back and away from his cock. When she raised glowing green eyes to his face in question, he stared down at her. With a muffled oath, he pushed her back on the bed and came over her, letting her feel the full weight of his body, the intensity of his need. Shifting underneath him, she felt his hard cock graze her sex and suddenly went still beneath him. Breathing heavily, he shifted his weight up onto his elbows and used his legs to push hers apart. Leaning down, he began kissing her frantically.

Sharon was overwhelmed. Liken's lower body was pressing into hers. His mouth was eating at hers like he was starving. She returned his kisses eagerly, wanting more, needing more of him. With a muffled moan into her mouth, he began to rub his cock against the outside of her sex. She was drowning in sensation. With an answering moan, she pressed her hips upward into his weight.

It took a second before she realized something else was happening as well. She could feel his mind pressing against hers. Even though he had done it before, it startled her enough to make her go still beneath him.

With a little moan, he breathed into her mouth, "Trust me, *sherree*...please — it will be so good..."

His hips pushed down against hers again, pantomiming the act they both craved. She pushed back, feeling bursts of pleasure at the friction of their bodies. He immediately adjusted his position so that the next time he pressed, his cock pressed at the entrance to her opening. She shook with desire and nerves. "I do want you..." She raised her hips.

His next thrust took him a little inside. He slowed his movement. "You are so tight. I will be careful..." With a gentle thrust, he moved further in. He could feel the tightness of her inner walls gently stretch to accommodate him.

Sharon felt his hardness filling her. She was stunned by what she felt. He was too big. She had to relax or it was going to be painful. She gasped and tried to ignore the pressing feeling of him in her head. She could feel the weight of his mind against hers like a tangible thing. It was scary. He seemed to be pushing into her body and into her mind at the same time. She was tensing up. She couldn't help it.

Liken slowed even further. His forehead was coated with sweat. He looked like he was in agony. "*Sherree*, stay with me... "His next thrust was firmer, making significant headway. He was nearly all the way inside her now.

She could see what his gentleness was costing him. With a deep breath, she consciously focused on relaxing her inner muscles. The press of his mind against hers had eased a little, which helped. The next thrust he went deeply, completely inside her. She gasped.

When he was in her to the hilt, they both stopped moving for a second. It was exquisite.

Sharon felt stretched and full. It was so incredible. For a moment she shut her eyes, just savoring the feel of him deep inside her. Then her eyes opened and locked on his in wonder.

Her look seemed to melt something inside him. His eyes lit and his mouth curved tenderly. Leaning down, he softly kissed her mouth. He began thrusting gently in and out of her.

Each thrust inward lit her on fire. She began to move with him. She wanted more. Eyes closing, head thrown back, she arched upward further, seeking the strength of his body. Her hips surged to meet his thrusts.

As if he had been waiting for that response, he arched his spine. His thrusts became harder, faster. With each thrust, she could feel his mind pressing harder against hers. His mind was probing at hers, just as his body was probing. Eyes opening in fear, she held his gaze as if her life depended upon it.

With a moan, he muttered, "Trust me. Please..."

At his plea, she felt something inside herself give. She did trust him. Suddenly, she felt a blinding pain in her head, as if someone had driven a spike through it. She screamed. "It hurts! Oh, god, it hurts!"

They both stopped moving. Tears sprang to her eyes, and she instinctively moved her hands up to her head. For a minute, all she could feel was the overwhelming pain. Then, gradually, she became aware of something else. Feelings, not her own, began to register. She could feel him in her mind like a wave. It was like he was moving through her. She could feel waves of concern and regret, but mixed with those a sense of satisfaction and possession.

His voice was gruff with concern. "Are you all right?"

Feeling a little hysterical, she shook her head no. She couldn't speak.

"Just relax for minute, *sherree*. All will be well. You have my oath on it."

Sharon could feel and hear his sincerity. His actual words suddenly penetrated. Oath was probably an unfortunate word choice at that moment. *It was their stupid oath that had gotten her into this…whatever this was,* she thought angrily.

Reaching down to place a gentle kiss on her lips, Liken said, "Maybe so, *sherree*, but I am grateful for that oath. I am grateful for you."

With a start of surprise, she realized he had known what she was thinking. She immediately wondered if he could read her mind all the time now. She was horrified at the thought.

With a little smile, he said, "Not *all* the time, *sherree*. I will never completely leave you, but you will have some privacy. To do otherwise would be unhealthy for both of us. Ahhh, you still feel horrified. Do not fear this merging, Sharon. There are a great many benefits for me to show you." He gently thrust into her body. "Let me show you."

A strong wave of pleasure caught her by surprise. She was feeling not only her own pleasure, but his as well. As his thrusts grew stronger, she arched her body in response.

With a little moan, he said, "Yes, that is it."

His thrusts increased in tempo. As she rose up to meet him, she felt waves of pleasure surging back and forth between them. It was impossible to separate the two sensations. With a groan, she pushed against him harder, wanting more.

He rose up on his elbows, gaining leverage. He was really surging into her hard, pulling back, then surging forward to the hilt again and again. It felt so incredible that she could barely breathe.

Looking down into her face, Liken muttered, "Merging allows me to know how you feel when I do this…" He pushed into her hard on the downstroke and used his hips to pin hers.

She felt the pressure on her clitoris and cried out in surprise and pleasure. His answering groan was deep and husky. He kept stroking her like that again and again, making the pressure inside both of them build higher and higher.

Without realizing it, her hands were running from his shoulders down his back all the way to his hips. She grabbed onto his ass and held on, her nails biting into him. The tiny pinpricks of pain nearly sent him over the edge. He slammed into her harder. With a muttered oath, he grabbed one of her hands and pulled it over her head, then quickly did the same with the opposite hand. Holding both arms over her head, he kept pounding into her.

With ruthless precision, he never lost rhythm. They were both moaning now. Sweat turned their bodies slick. Driving into her, he stared down into her face. Between gasps of air, he said, "Go over…just give into it…no more control, *sherree*…only this…" He was rough, demanding, pushing her even harder.

All the tension building inside her seemed to tighten in that moment. With a scream, she let loose, feeling her body contract and then release over and over again. Waves of pleasure poured through her, sending her higher.

As her inner muscles milked him, he moaned loudly, still pumping. Her pleasure sent him right over the edge. With an even louder groan, he exploded, spewing into her. She could feel his warmth inside her as the waves of his pleasure suddenly hit her, too. She was blind with pleasure, deaf with it. For a moment, the two of them were locked together in shared pleasure, unsure who was feeling exactly what and not really caring. It was intense, unbelievable.

When the feelings began to fade, he seemed to suddenly realize he was leaning on her heavily. He carefully twisted to lie on his back, bringing her up against him. With her head on his chest, his hand rubbing her back, both of them focused on simply breathing. Eventually, the gasping sounds of their breaths ceased and the room grew quiet.

Sharon tried to make some sense out of what had just happened. It had been incredibly intense, unlike anything she had ever experienced. Sex was not like whatever this had been. This was something else.

Liken's voice broke the silence. "It was not sex, Sharon. It was merging. And it was incredible."

Sharon entire body went stiff. The hands on her back never faltered, just continued with their soothing motions. "I thought you wouldn't be able to read my mind all the time." Her voice held accusation as well as hurt. She rose up a little to see his face.

With a little grimace, he shook his head. "You misunderstood. I said you would have some privacy, *sherree*. It is not that I cannot read your mind all the time. It is more that I will not."

"Well, stop then." She was getting freaked out. "Wait a minute...you can do this anytime, even if I'm not in the same room with you? Even if..."

His voice was patient. "Yes, even if you go back to Earth. I would like to remind you, though, that you will not be going back to Earth. Do you honestly think we are not compatible after this?" His eyes were beginning to glitter with anger.

He was angry, but underneath that, he was worried about losing her. Sharon realized she could feel his emotions quite clearly. She didn't have any trouble separating what he was feeling from what she was feeling. There was some distance now. It was different than it had been when they were having sex, more clearly defined. Hmmm. He could read her mind, but she could read his emotions. That might prove interesting.

"I didn't say we weren't compatible sexually. But there's more to a relationship than sex." Her mouth turned up at the corners in a sleepy little smile. "Even if it is great sex."

Going along with her lighter tone for the moment, Liken consciously relaxed his shoulders. "Of course." His voice held lazy male satisfaction. "Great sex, friendship, great sex, respect, great sex, liking, and then, of course, there is great sex. I did mention that one, did I not?" His smile was teasing.

She shook her head in mock surprise. "I believe that's the first I've heard of it. And to think I held the belief that men are shallow creatures with no clue about what's important in a relationship." Her eyes were lit with laughter, but her lids were falling. She was trying to stay awake, but it was a losing battle.

With great tenderness his hand moved from her shoulder to the back of her head. "I think I do not have the energy left for this debate nor do you." With a gentle push, he moved her head back onto his chest. "You are exhausted, *sherree*. Let us rest now. Tomorrow is soon enough to discuss male flaws."

Unconsciously rubbing her cheek against his chest, she relaxed into the gentle feel of his hands moving soothingly over her back. She let out a little sigh. "Liken…"

Her voice was so soft he would not have heard her without his extraordinary hearing. "Yes?"

"It was beautiful, wasn't it?" Her voice faded a little with each word. Her lids closed as she drifted off.

Reaching down to place a soft kiss on her head, he whispered, "Yes, *sherree*, it was beautiful."

He lay there in the dim room seeing images of Sharon in his mind. Sharon standing across from him as they made their oath. Sharon staring at the portal, her eyes wide with fear and courage. Sharon at the table eating, biting into the yellow *rerha* fruit, her grimace comical as she quickly put it back onto her plate. Sharon coming apart in his arms, in his bed.

With a sigh of his own, he reduced the room to darkness, and ignored the renewing ache in his body. The merging had been beautiful. But it was not just her physical beauty and their passion that had made it so incredible. It was her inner beauty as they joined that had brought such joy. He would never grow tired of experiencing the wonder of her.

They were going to be very happy together. She could not leave him. He would do whatever he must to make sure of it. Her comment about males being shallow echoed in his mind.

His last thought before sleep claimed him rang with determination. He might be shallow, but stupid he was not. He would find a way to keep her.

Chapter Seven

The next morning, Sharon hesitated in the doorway of the kitchen area. Liken had his back to her. He was once again dressed in black, although he was barefoot. He was reaching into an oblong recessed area, gathering fruit from inside, and then placing them in a bowl. There was a panel with buttons to the left. When he had gathered enough, he pressed one of the buttons and a small section of the wall slid back in place.

The Shimerian version of refrigeration or food transport, she guessed. She waited for him to turn as she gathered her composure. What exactly were the Shimerian rules of behavior for the morning after? She pasted a polite smile on her face and decided she could bluff her way through it. She was calm. She was sophisticated. He turned and spotted her in the doorway. She was in trouble.

She felt heat climb into her cheeks. "Do you ever wear anything but black?" The words all ran together and her voice was too high. She cringed inwardly. She hadn't meant to sound critical.

His eyes glinted with some unnamed thought. He said, "It denotes my profession. Only guardians are allowed to wear black." His voice teased her gently as he added, "Should we talk of footwear next or would you come greet me properly?"

Feeling foolish, she walked over and gave him a quick kiss on the lips. She kept the bowl between them and moved back too quickly for him to grab her. Walking back toward the table, she could see it was already set. There were beautiful flowers of some kind resting in a vase in the center. There were cups by each plate and a pitcher next to the flowers.

Her voice was very serious in an attempt to remain composed. She didn't want him to realize how deeply nervous she was feeling. "Can I help with anything?"

She looked like she was facing an angry death squad instead of her lover. He responded with equal gravity, although he felt like laughing. The urge to tease her was almost irresistible. "No, but I appreciate your offer of assistance. I am merely placing this bowl on the table and we will be ready."

She sat down in the seat before he could assist her and watched him put the bowl on the table. She scooted her chair into place and placed a small cloth from the table into her lap. He sat down across from her. With a little nod of his head, he gestured to the bowl. "Please take whatever you desire."

Her gaze flew to his face, but his tone was innocent. Deciding to give him the benefit of the doubt, she studied the fruit. Immediately she noticed there were no bitter yellow ones. Picking up a purple and red one that she remembered was pretty tasty, she took a bite. It was strangely salty for a fruit, but pleasant.

Again in that same overly innocent tone, he said, "It is indeed fortunate that you enjoy salty flavors." His eyes were devilish.

She choked. "Okay. Enough. I haven't had breakfast yet. I'm not up to mind reading and double entendres. I've had that bloodbath of a shower, but I need caffeine. What are the odds that you have coffee?" She wasn't annoyed but his teasing wasn't helping her frayed nerves.

He smiled. "I am sorry, but we do not have coffee." He gestured to the opaque cup in front of her. "We do have *ykanze* juice. It is very refreshing."

She peered suspiciously at the dark green liquid in the cup. "It looks like cough medicine." When he laughed, she took a cautious sip. It was surprising good. The liquid was hot and a little spicy. It tasted somewhat like a Bloody Mary. She felt the heat as it made its way to her stomach. "Is it alcoholic?"

He shook his head. "No, it is not fermented. It is also not addictive, although many claim it unthinkable to begin the day without it."

"I like it." Her voice reflected her surprise. "It's different, but it's good."

He looked as if he wanted to tease her again. At her discouraging look, he merely shrugged and began eating. The two of them ate in companionable silence for a while. She concentrated on her food in a conscious effort to avoid thinking too hard. When she finished, she looked up to find him watching her. "What?" she said, a little apprehensively.

"I am merely enjoying the sight of you this day, *sherree*." His gaze roamed her body with possessive satisfaction. "I have fantasized about you for so long. It is still a wonder to have you here."

Straightening in her seat, she decided it was time to take control of the situation before sex clouded things. With as much firmness as she could muster, she said, "We need to talk."

He winced. She guessed those words struck fear into the heart of any man, regardless of home planet. With a resigned shrug, he nodded his head. Sharon was relieved at his agreement. It was time to get some answers. She had been avoiding some things and he had deliberately distracted her about others. That was going to change. She was a librarian. Information was knowledge. Knowledge was power. Where to begin?

She remembered his comment at the portal. It had been nagging at her since that time. "What did you mean when you said you knew about me a year ago?" She wiped her face with the cloth from her lap.

"I found you telepathically a year ago." Liken paused, searching for the best way to make her understand. "You would have experienced it as a kind of daydream. I had been reaching out to you since my twentieth year and then suddenly, you were there. My mind brushed yours."

"How old are you?" What if Shimerians aged differently? She hadn't thought to ask about it until now. He could be much older or younger than her, she thought.

"I am the equivalent of thirty-four Earth years." He answered her unspoken thought. "Earth years and Shimerian years are roughly the same. I was thirty-three when I found you."

She thought about that for a minute. "Why did you wait?" She quickly tried to correct that. "I mean, not that I'm complaining or anything. I'm curious."

His gaze were steady on hers. "You were not ready, Sharon. I knew the adjustments you would have to make would be very hard. I wanted to give you time. Time to yourself. When I connected with you, I saw your image of your future."

When she merely continued to stare at him in confusion, he elaborated. "You think of yourself as very ordinary. You are cautious by nature. You value safety and control. The future you envisioned was very comfortable — your job at the library, a few good friends, a very ordinary man who would love you, one or two children. Nothing extraordinary. No trips to foreign planets. No alien pactmates. Nothing too different from the safe life you were leading. You did not want adventure, Sharon. You did not want disruption and challenge and a new culture. In short, you did not want a life with me." His voice held no hint of hurt, merely stated the facts.

She let out a breath in protest. "Okay. Thanks for making me sound like the dullest woman on Earth. If you were so convinced that I didn't want a life with you, then why wait a year and then summon me to oath? I don't get it."

He considered her words. "I waited to give you as much time as I could in that safe life. I want you to be happy, Sharon. You may not admit it now, but that safe life you were leading was growing boring."

She thought it over. She had been growing restless of late. Over the last couple of years, she had begun to wonder what was missing in her orderly life. She had felt a kind of wistfulness for something more. She had never managed to figure out exactly what *more* entailed, but she had been conscious of it. However, that didn't mean she had been yearning for adventure on quite this scale. "What if I had married one of those ordinary men, huh?" Her tone was challenging.

His look was fierce. "You would not have pledged with another man after we connected. Our destiny was decided in that moment."

"So, what does that mean? You thought you'd give me time to grow bored? And then rescue me from my idiotic little life, is that it?" She was getting angry. Could he be any more insulting?

"I am not trying to insult you. I am merely explaining. You needed time to see that the path you were taking would not make you happy. You needed time to yourself so that you could adjust to all of the changes later." He was losing patience. She was trying to distance the two of them.

She could feel his irritation. It was strange to be so closely attuned to someone, even when arguing. She wasn't sure what to make of it. She tried for a placating tone. "I don't want to fight. I'm just not sure I like you being the one to make that kind of a decision about my life. I make my own decisions."

He challenged bluntly, "Would you have wished for me to claim you a year ago?"

She considered the question honestly. "No, I guess you're right. I probably would have been even more freaked out then than I am now."

Her agreement calmed him. "I was aiming for your happiness then, *sherree*. As I aim for it now."

With a little nod, she acknowledged his words. "I appreciate that. I believe you mean it. I just don't like the feeling that you were waiting in the background, calling all the shots."

He looked a little puzzled at the statement. Then understanding seemed to hit. "I see. I understand, but it was the correct thing to do at the time."

"Okay. Let's put that aside for a minute. What do you mean you connected with me a year ago?" Could he have known about her for a year without her being aware of it? The thought unsettled her. Just how much did he know about her?

Liken sensed her growing unease and decided a full explanation might help her. "Perhaps I should explain some other things first. Shimerian males, from the time they begin school, learn Shimerian and Earth cultures. Our studies included Earth languages, customs, ideas. It was a preparation for our future. At the same time, we learn how to focus our mental abilities."

Her attention was caught. She interrupted. "What exactly are those abilities?"

Liken chose his words carefully. "Some of it is difficult to explain. We can harness mental energy and convert it to other types of energy. In that way, I was able to control the light mechanism this morning. I confess, however, that I do not have much of what you would call telekinetic ability. Also, we are able to reach out with our minds and touch the minds of others. We can all shield against others to a certain degree, but it varies according to individual abilities. For instance, I am a high degree shielder, but I am even better at probing."

She could attest to that. Memories of him thrusting into her last night swamped her. The thought brought a blush to her face.

His expression reflected his amusement at her thoughts. "By probing I mean getting information from another. It is very helpful in my profession. When I need to question someone, even if they are uncooperative, I am able to get the information I need." He was not boasting. He was considered to be one of the best probers in his section.

She could see how that would be a huge advantage with a suspect. So much for the right to remain silent. "Your English is very good. Have you used probing to help with that?"

He looked pleased with her compliment. "Yes. The schooling we received was effective, but a lot of Earth expressions are very confusing. Your slang is quite colorful. Probing has been very helpful in understanding it."

She considered his words. "Of course, to be exposed to slang... Have you been to Earth before?" She didn't know why she found the idea so surprising.

"Yes, of course. I have been to Earth many times. To many of your different countries. You have a great variety of cultures. It is quite amazing." He smiled at the thought of his visits to Earth. They had been quite educational and highly entertaining.

"Wow." She suddenly realized something that should have been obvious. She knew from last night that he was a very experienced lover. There weren't many unattached Shimerian women. So he must have been having sex with...

He raised his eyebrows. "I have found your people to be very friendly. Earth females in particular seem to find Shimerian travelers quite exotic. Although I was never able to stay long, I developed many... friendships...during my stays on your world."

The emphasis nearly made her snort. She'd bet on it. She had seen Shimerian males before, of course. Although she personally had never had much contact with them, she had never paid much attention in the past. Other than their good looks and larger size, most of them pretty much blended in with the surrounding culture. Just ordinary travelers touring the city or out having a good time. Probably, she conceded to herself, too big and powerful looking for her to want to cross paths with them much either.

Looking back, she realized none of them seemed to be lacking in female companionship. She suddenly pictured Liken out having a good time with some other woman. She frowned.

His past was none of her business she told herself firmly. For that matter, after the knowing period, it was no concern of hers if he slept with someone else. Right? Her heart gave a pang at the thought.

He looked pleased. "There is no need for jealousy, *sherree*. I want only to be with you now. We are merged."

"Stop doing that!" she said sharply. "Stay out of my head. You said I could have some privacy. It's not right for you to just march into my thoughts and read them like today's newspaper."

This was the part of the discussion he had hoped to avoid. He knew it would put them in conflict, but he did not want dishonesty between them. "I cannot completely leave you, Sharon. Our minds have been merged." He tried to find a way to make her understand the truth of it.

She was indignant. "Oh, that's just great! Don't you have some control over this thing?"

He felt his patience strain at her tone. "Yes, I have some control. But a part of me is always with you. I can withdraw to a certain degree, but when you are agitated, as you are now, it is..."

He tried to think of a way she would understand. "It is like having the volume of a radio turned to the maximum level. You broadcast. I cannot help but listen. After a time, I will become better at blocking you, but it will be helpful when you become better at not broadcasting."

He was reading her every thought. This was not good. She needed to calm down. She could feel his growing impatience pressing against her in waves. She was in over her head. She should be coping with overdue fines or putting away books on their proper shelves. She was a librarian, for goodness sake. She liked order, and quiet, and calm. She was a reserved, quiet kind of person. This was all too...chaotic. Her life had turned inside out-alien planets, mind merging, incredible sex.

She let out a little breath. "All right. I'll try not to broadcast. You try to stay out as much as possible, okay? I don't like the idea of you snooping around in my mind, knowing every little thing..."

As she thought of the possibilities, she suddenly felt very vulnerable. He would be able to know everything. Not that she had a lot of dark secrets, but she was human, after all. She had things she would never tell another person. Things she wasn't particularly proud to share with someone else. Fantasies in the dark of the night she wouldn't even share with a sexual partner. The whole idea filled her with intense discomfort.

He looked apologetic, but there was heat in his eyes as well. "I am trying to respect your wishes, Sharon, but you are becoming even more upset. There should be no shame or embarrassment between us. I know your inner self. It is incredible to me that you can be so blind to your own beauty, both physical and inner."

Reaching across the table to take her hand, his voice became husky. "I would not use our bond against you, *sherree*. I do not wish to hurt you. Anything I have learned from our sharing will be used only for your pleasure and mine." His thumb was gently stroking her hand.

Her gaze slid from his and she tried to pull her hand from his grasp. She still felt incredibly exposed. He knew too much. She needed some space to come to terms with what he'd told her. With obvious reluctance, he let her pull away completely.

She promptly scooted as far back as her chair would allow. She tried to turn the subject to safer channels. She decided to go on the offensive. "I know you've been with other women before. You've had sex without merging. Why last night?" *And why me* she wanted to add, but didn't quite have the nerve.

"You are my pactmate, my future pledgemate." At her instinctive movement to disagree he flashed her a fierce look. "I could have had sex without merging with you, it is true. I tried to wait. The initial merge is somewhat painful and frightening to the female. Some choose to merge right after the Oath. I tried to be patient. I thought it might be easier when you knew me better. I also waited as long as I could out of prudence. You were not happy with the Oath. I thought you might have even greater problems with the consequences of merging." His tone said he had been right.

"But you could have held off, right? I mean, this merging business is permanent. Even after we go our separate ways, you'll still be lurking in the back of my mind!" The more she thought about it, the angrier she felt. Once again, he had taken a choice out of her hands. After knowing her for only two days, he had simply decided that the time was right and linked them together permanently.

His frustration pushed back at her. His face grew harsh. For a minute he stared at her in silence. Then, as if coming to some decision, he spoke. His voice was too controlled, almost cold. "I see I have been taking the wrong approach with you all this time. I thought easing you into our new life would be best. Now I think it is time for you to confront reality and accept that your life has changed permanently. There are things you do not know yet."

Angrily, she pushed her chair back and stood. "Oh, now is the time for me to face reality, huh?" Her voice was sarcastic. "In what other ways are you planning to disrupt my life? Let's see…you could take me from my home and my friends and my job? Oh yeah," Her resentment was making her chest tight. "You've already done that. How about you invade my privacy by reading my innermost thoughts? Oh, that's right. You've done that, too."

Her voice broke and she had to swallow. Her tone softened. "I think I've faced plenty of your reality, thanks very much. I don't care what other surprises are around the corner. I've had enough of your reality."

Still seated, he looked up at her. Very softly he said, "Sit down." His tone demanded complete obedience.

When she didn't immediately respond, but continued to stare at him, he said, "You claim I have been making your choices for you. You do not wish to be treated as a child with no say in its future. Sit down and I will explain what choices you have at this time."

She could tell that he was out of patience. She could feel his anger like a living thing in the room. Holding his gaze, she carefully sat back down in her chair. "Fine. Explain."

"How many pactmates do you think file incompatible?" he asked in a conversational tone completely at odds with his expression.

She was caught off guard by the question and tone. "I don't know. I've heard that there aren't many, but I really don't know." She couldn't remember any statistics if she had ever even learned them.

"Not many." He nodded his head. His hard gaze still on her face, he continued. "One could say not many. More accurately, one should say none. There has never been an incompatible filing."

In total shock, she wondered whether he was telling the truth. "That doesn't make sense. Somewhere along the way, there had to have been some." She couldn't keep the disbelief out of her voice.

"No, Sharon, there have not been any. When a Shimerian male connects with his mate, it is not some kind of accident. He has been searching for a particular female, one that matches him mind and body. Why he is able to find her at a certain time and not before, that is a mystery. By the number of unattached males still seeking mates, you can understand that many spend years waiting and searching."

His whole body leaned forward as he said sincerely, "No one understands why it happens when it happens. But the truth is, once he connects with her, he recognizes his mate. There can be no other. Because his mind has touched hers, she unconsciously knows he is out there. She does not know his name or who he is, but the idea of that mate is there. She knows there is someone just for her. She cannot settle for less."

He watched as the anger drained from her face. "You understand what I am saying because you have felt it yourself."

Ignoring the building confusion in her expression, he continued. "We are mated in a way that cannot be denied. Our merging was inevitable. Our lives are intertwined and will never be separate again. You may fight against it or refuse to acknowledge it, but it will not change what will happen. It is convenient that you were on the register. If you had not been registered, I would have found you and taken you. It would have been more difficult, but I would have gotten you here in the end. We are meant to be together. You can fight me, but you cannot fight yourself or the rightness of our mating."

They sat there in silence as she digested his words. His anger was cooling, but there was a new hardness to his resolve.

In a subdued tone, she said, "I don't know what to think anymore. I can't seem to get my feet under me before you pull out the rug again." She rubbed a weary hand across her forehead. She looked into his eyes. "You're saying neither of us had a choice. That our coming together was cosmic destiny or something." Her eyes seemed to be begging him to help her understand.

His expression eased a little. "Cosmic destiny? Perhaps." Maybe she was truly beginning to accept. He knew she did not completely believe, but it was a beginning. It was time to show her their compatibility before she tried to distance herself again.

Standing up, he held out his hand. "Come, Sharon. We have talked as you requested. There is no need to spoil the entire suntime with weighty matters."

When she did not put her hand in his immediately, he walked around the table and took her by the arm. She stood up, but pulled free from his grasp quickly. Her action wasn't intended to insult, but he felt that way.

"Enough! Still you pull away. It is always the same. You run from me. You run from yourself. No more." With a tug, he pulled her into his arms.

She pushed back from him as much as she could in protest. "I'm not running!" She didn't want to prove him right so she forced herself to be still. "I'm thinking about what you've said."

"We are through with this talk," he muttered just before his mouth closed over hers. His kiss was demanding, giving her no choice but to respond. Under the hard pressure of his lips, her mouth opened and he thrust his tongue greedily inside. With a little moan, he pulled her tightly against him.

Her body remembered the wee hours of the night, even if her mind had been trying to block the memories. With a groan of her own, she pressed closer, enjoying the feel of his hard body. The kiss continued, steadily growing hotter, wetter. Her arms moved up his chest.

With an impatient noise, he reached under her bottom, pulling her up so that his hardness pressed into the notch between her thighs. Drowning in sensation, she wrapped her legs around his waist. His cock pushed against the heated softness of her sex, and they both stilled in pure enjoyment.

Then, with determination, he began walking down the hallway. Each step was pure sensual torture. By the time they reached the bedroom, he felt as if his cock was going to burst before he could get inside her. Sitting down on the bed, he placed her standing in front of him.

As she looked down into his face, she realized there was no point in trying to resist him. She could fight him, but she couldn't fight what he made her feel. With her surrender came another realization. This would be no patient, gentle union. His eyes were black with desire. His hands were rough as he pulled her blouse over her head and tossed it to the floor. He leaned forward immediately. His hungry mouth latched on to an aching nipple and he sucked it hard into his mouth.

Her mind shut down completely. She groaned and arched her back, feeling the delicious pull, wanting more. Her hands went to the back of his head and held him there. For the next minute he greedily sucked, pausing only to lick or gently bite. His hands roamed from her back to her hips covered only by a thin skirt and panties. He began kneading, flexing his fingers into her soft flesh.

He switched to her other breast, giving it the same attention. She was burning up from the wet heat of his mouth and tongue. With a little whimper, she shifted her weight from one leg to the other, conscious of the aching heat between her thighs. She felt overwhelmed with pleasure, out of control with need. Her hands were equally rough as she reached down and pulled his shirt over his head.

The muscular strength of his chest gleamed. She ran her hands over it, pausing to tease the flat nubs of his nipples. The answering jump of flexing muscles under her hands indicated his pleasure at her touch. She started to climb onto his lap.

Before she could get on top of him, he pushed her back. She paused in confusion. With a pained grin, he shook his head, stood up, and bent to remove his pants. In response, she reached down and quickly removed her skirt and panties.

Feeling his hungry gaze on her as he sat back down, she felt self-conscious suddenly. Holding the panties and skirt in her hand, she straightened. Gathering her courage, she looked into his face.

What she saw there surprised her. There was desire and approval, but more than that, there was need. He looked nearly as out of control as she felt. With more confidence, she threw the clothing to the floor and stood there proudly in front of him.

His gaze roamed her body, from her hair to her toes in a near physical caress. His obvious admiration made her feel powerful. He wanted her badly. He had wanted her for over a year. Swallowing past the dryness in her throat, she said, "I want you right now."

Heavy lidded, his gaze returned to her face. "Then take me, *sherree*." He reached out and helped her straddle his waist. Her knees were over his thighs, her breasts even with his mouth. Reaching down, she found his hard cock and ran her hand up and down it in a fisted motion.

He dug his hands into the sheets. His head went back and she licked the sweaty line of his throat. Balancing so that his cock was at the very edge of her entrance, she paused. His hands came to her hips.

With a shake of her head, she said, "No, I'm taking you, remember?" She was going to be in control this time around.

His head came forward and glazed eyes met hers. "This time, *sherree*. This time." Reaching a hand forward to toy with her clitoris, he said, "But I can induce you to hurry."

With a muffled moan, she slid down onto his cock halfway, before control reasserted. She used her hand and to push his hand away from her. Placing her palms on his shoulders, she levered her body back up. Staring into his face, she sank back down, slowly, inch-by-inch. Then she pulled back up with that same slow movement.

Feeling heat suffuse her body, she realized quickly that in torturing him, she was torturing herself. With each movement upward, his hard flesh rasped against the sensitive nerves of her inner muscles. As she slid back down, the pleasure flared, his hard cock filling the empty ache.

He let her control the pace, feel her own power, and satisfy her own need. This was a fantasy of hers that he had known would be delicious torment. He knew it was only a matter of time until his control broke. Her movements were growing faster. As her tight sex squeezed his aching cock, he felt the pressure building at the base of his spine.

Like the too-tight stretch of a rubber band, his control broke. He said in a hard voice, "No more."

His hands came around her like steel bands and his fingers dug into her hips. He began lifting her up and then pushing her down as he arched upward inside her.

Her nails dug into his shoulders as she lost control of her motions. He leaned forward as far as he could and began licking her nipples, teasing those hard points as if he had never tasted anything so sweet.

Between his mouth at her breast and the hard stroke of his cock, Sharon lost control. She blindly followed his guiding hands, any thought lost in a haze of need. She could only feel the rise and fall of her own body. Her focus narrowed down to the building pressure of her throbbing sex. She felt the tension gathering, her body tightening in anticipation of the coming pleasure. With a frustrated whimper, she breathed, "I'm going to come…"

She was taken by complete surprise when Liken thrust fully into her mind. He filled her head, his pleasure mingling and then multiplying her own. Screaming his name, she clung helplessly as the tension in her body broke. The pulsing contractions of her body went on and on as wave after wave of release flooded her senses.

She heard his strangled moan as her orgasm pushed him over the last edge of control. He erupted inside her, pouring into her, his entire body shaking in release. His hands on her hips were bruising, but she was barely aware of the pain. Her head fell limply on his shoulder, her entire body relaxed and heavy with exhaustion. She couldn't move. She didn't even want to move. They remained in that position for several minutes.

Finally, she lifted her head back off his shoulder and pulled back to see his face, unaware of the sensual picture she made at that moment. Her hair was a tousled mess, her face rosy and sweaty from exertion. Her eyes were glowing with satisfaction as she smiled and said, "So maybe there are some advantages to merging."

With a sense of surprise, Liken realized he wanted her all over again. Within minutes of the most powerful orgasm of his life, he was already beginning to harden inside her. As her eyes widened in shock, he wrapped a hand in her tousled hair and began pulling her head forward for a kiss. Shaking his head in mock disagreement, his lips curved as he said, "You will have to prove it to me, *sherree*."

She answered his mock serious tone. "Well, if I must, I must. I am ever obedient."

He couldn't contain a snort of disbelief at that statement. His quiet, docile little librarian was incredibly strong-willed.

Pressing her mouth to his, she teasingly nipped his bottom lip and then gave it a conciliatory lick. She was enjoying their play.

Catching the back of her head more firmly, he spoke against her lips. "Obedient you are not…but I can be patient for a time." He grinned widely and watched as fire began to fill her eyes. To prevent her from answering, he began to actively kiss her. As the tone of the kiss began to change from playful to hungry, any response flew from her mind.

Many hours later they emerged from the bedroom motivated by the need for food. They were both passion-drunk and nearly reeling, but their faces were mirrors of happy satisfaction. Issues like destined pledgemates, incompatibility filings, and obedience were pushed away in exploration of their mutual pleasure in each other. For a brief time.

Chapter Eight

For the rest of the week, Sharon tried to keep an open mind. She wasn't sure that she believed the whole destined mate theory, but she was willing to give it a chance. Her attraction to Liken was more powerful than anything she could ever have imagined. Maybe they could love each other. She didn't like the idea of leaving Earth, but she decided to consider what living on Shimeria could mean. Maybe they could be happy together. Liken had taken great pains to show her the advantages of a life on Shimeria with him.

Each day he took her on explorations of his home world. They went to museums, restaurants, and even shopping. The "commerce centers" as he called shops were especially fun. Her face heated and she felt the warmth of desire wash over her as she remembered that trip. It had started out innocently enough when he asked if she would enjoy some shopping. They had wandered into a commerce center in the business district. Walking into the feminine shop, she thought he looked out-of-place and adorable as he seriously considered the women's clothes.

The shop had a range of colors and sizes, but the outfits were pretty similar to the ones she wore. Like most shops on Earth, the clothing hung from racks. Sharon spied a female clerk toward the back of the shop and was surprised to note that she was human. She was tall and thin, with her blonde hair pulled back into a classic bun. The female clerk came forward, eyeing him appreciatively. "May I assist you, *Isshalee*? "

Sharon bristled a little at her tone and look, but Liken appeared not to notice. He answered her seriously. "My pactmate would like to purchase some garments. It must be something special, to match her beauty."

Reluctantly turning her attention to Sharon, the clerk studied her thoughtfully for a moment. "I am sure that we can find something for you, *Isshal*." Walking over to a rack filled with outfits, she drew out a halter of shimmering blue, with a very short skirt and panties to match. "I believe this will compliment your eyes and fair complexion quite well."

Sharon studied the length doubtfully. "I don't know. It looks a little short." It certainly didn't look like something a librarian would wear on Earth.

Liken laughed. "I believe it will look incredible on you, *sherree*. Why don't you try it on?" He wanted to see her expression when she saw herself in the outfit. Even more than her expression, he wanted to see her long legs and full breasts in that little shirt and short skirt.

Nodding uncertainly, Sharon agreed. She was trying all kinds of new things these days. She might as well go with the flow. Following the clerk into a back area of the shop, she saw that there were a series of buttons along the wall about every six feet. As the clerk pushed one, the section slid back to reveal a dressing room.

Sharon walked in and turned to get the outfit from the clerk. She was stunned to find Liken right behind her, holding the outfit. He walked through and the section slid shut behind him. She asked, "What are you doing in here?"

Liken lifted a brow. He thought it was obvious. "I'm here to watch you try on the outfit, *sherree*."

She watched him place the clothes on a hook in one wall and then sit in a chair in the far right corner. There were no mirrors to be seen. This planet was bizarre. "You mean they don't have mirrors here? I'm just supposed to rely on your opinion?"

He laughed. Pressing a button on the wall next to the chair, Liken waited for her reaction. Her astonished expression as the hologram emerged was priceless.

Sharon was staring at a three-dimensional hologram of herself. As she moved, the image moved with her, reflecting her actions. It was very lifelike, looking real enough to give her the feeling that there were three of them in the room, although two of them looked exactly alike. She cautiously moved around the room, trying to figure out where the hologram would end. As she reached Liken's chair, the image faded abruptly. She exclaimed, "That is so weird. It's so real!"

He laughed again. "Indeed it is. As you can see, we have no need for mirrors. You can see for yourself using the hologram how the clothing looks."

Sharon realized he expected her to change in front of him. He had already seen every part of her naked, she reminded herself. There was no reason to be awkward about it. Resolutely, she pulled her blouse over her head and heard Liken's breath catch in his throat.

Gaze jumping to his, she saw the raw desire heat his gaze immediately. He looked at her breasts, and she felt her nipples tighten in a tingling rush of response. Embarrassment be damned, she decided. He was looking at her like he couldn't get enough of the sight. Holding the blouse in one hand, she walked toward him and handed it to him.

He took it automatically and set it on the floor beside him, although his gaze moved to her face. She knew what that look meant. She was not having sex in a dressing room. She stepped away from him and reached for her skirt, conscious of his gaze on her. Still, it might be fun to tease him a little. She felt her own blood heat at the thought.

Liken watched as Sharon turned her back to him and began to slide the skirt over her hips, slowly. Did she have any idea how crazy she was making him? He read her thoughts, finding them a jumble of conflicting needs, desires, and ideas. He couldn't sort them out. When she turned around, he saw the triumph and feminine power in her expression and decided she knew exactly how he felt.

He smiled in appreciation and settled back in the chair to enjoy the game. Pasting a calm expression on his face, he tried to appear disinterested. He shifted in the chair as his hard cock throbbed in direct dispute of his efforts.

Sharon wasn't fooled. She searched his face as she walked toward him clad only in panties, a pair of slender sandals, and a smile. She could feel the pleasant hum of arousal coursing through her. She could feel his gaze roam her body from her head to her toes, lingering on her face, breasts, and those tiny panties.

She was getting to him. Tossing the skirt, she stepped back again and reached for one of the bows holding the sides of her panties together. His gaze followed her hand and she saw him swallow.

Abruptly moving her hand away from the panties, she turned her back to him and bent over. She had to clear her throat once, before her husky voice would emerge. "I'd better take off the shoes. They don't match the new outfit." Her position hid her knowing smile.

Liken clinched the arms of the chair until his knuckles grew white. She was giving him an excellent view of her round ass, enticingly curved under the small panties. He wanted to stand up, rip the panties off, and plunge his cock into her wet heat from behind. She was going to get the fuck of her life if she kept playing with him like this.

Having removed her sandals, Sharon stood up and turned to face Liken again. Her gaze went from his hungry face to his whitened knuckles on the arms of the chairs. He was barely in control. There was something so arousing about undressing in front of a fully clothed man, watching your every move.

She began to imagine what it would be like if they actually had sex now in the dressing room. She looked at the bulging cock tenting his pants and felt wet with the idea of having him inside her. Some demon was driving her now. She was caught up in the game as much as he was, maybe more. She wanted to feel his hands and his mouth on her body.

Her breasts were aching, the nipples sensitive. Unconsciously, one hand came forward, lightly touching her mound through the panties and then moving from her stomach upward in a caressing motion, stopping at her breasts. When she rubbed one hard nipple, she realized suddenly what she was doing.

Jerking her hand back to her side, she tried to regain a little control. She would never have sex in a public place. It was highly inappropriate. Someone might see them or hear them. Even as she reminded herself of that fact, she felt her arousal grow. She wanted to make him crazy. She wanted to see if she could drive him past that phenomenal control.

Liken gave a strangled moan and shook his head as if clearing it. When he spoke, his voice was pure temptation. "You have forgotten that I am in your mind, *sherree*. Your fantasies are quite intriguing. I do not share your reservations. Don't you want to know what it would be like? Take the panties off for me and I will show you. I will touch and taste you exactly as you imagine. Take them off." His tone started as a sultry request and ended as an order.

She hesitated. Reaching down, she pulled one string and felt the knot come undone. His face grew harsher, a flush washing over his cheekbones. Swallowing past the lump in her throat and disregarding the inner voice whispering caution, she lightly tugged the second string and felt the panties fall to her feet.

Liken stared at the curly hair of her sex for one long moment. Abruptly standing up, he watched her eyes widen as his hands went to his pants. With rough movements, he shoved open the buttons until his straining cock sprung free. Pressing the button to activate the hologram, he stalked toward her.

Sharon felt a wave of apprehension. He looked savage. Seeing a sudden hologram of herself at that moment was a shock, even as the hologram changed to become both of them. He stalked around her until he was behind her, his hands coming up to grip her shoulders so that they faced the hologram together.

She saw an image of contrasts. Her fair skin, although flushed, looked pale in comparison to his darker complexion. His hands looked huge on her shoulders. Her eyes were heavy-lidded and dark. Her breasts were full with hardened nipples thrusting outward, as if begging for his touch.

He loomed behind her, his face etched in lines of aroused hunger. She watched with fascination as his masculine hands closed over her breasts and began to massage. She moaned at the sensation and leaned into his touch.

The woman in the hologram did the same. Liken spoke in a seductive whisper next to her ear. "It is like making love while watching another couple. Or maybe like another couple watching us as we make love."

Sharon shuddered at the arousing thought. He knew exactly how to make her crazy. This whole thing was crazy. She tried to regain some control.

She stepped back, but that brought her along the hard length of his body. She could feel his shirt and pants against her nakedness. She felt his cock press against her lower back and the top of her ass. She wanted him so much it was nearly painful.

Liken moved one hand to her sex and began caressing her heat. She was soaking wet. With a quiet hum of approval he played, teasing and circling her clit. He felt her weight sag against him. The couple in the hologram echoed their movements. It was all too much for him to withstand. He was tired of being patient.

Roughly turning her, he placed her back against the left wall. His mouth latched onto one nipple, sucking roughly. Sharon moaned and looked down at him, but then her eyes were drawn back to the hologram. She watched the man's cheeks cave in as he sucked, nearly swallowing the woman's breast. The answering pull on her own breast nearly burnt her alive.

Liken lifted her by the hips with her back to the wall and then paused with her above his cock. Lowering her, he felt her sultry heat swallow him. He slid into her wetness and sank to the hilt. As their bodies merged, he merged his mind with hers. Her legs came around him to cling to his waist.

He pulled out and then thrust into her again. Sharon's head fell back against the wall. He could hear the thoughts in her mind, feel their pleasure building with each stroke. He paused, still buried in her heat.

Leaning forward, he whispered, "Remember, *sherree*, you must be quiet. If you are not quiet, the clerk will hear you."

Sharon tensed at his words. She had forgotten her surroundings. They shouldn't be doing this here. She realized her hands were clinging to his shoulders, her fingers digging into the silky material, and tried to push against his shoulders. She began to protest softly, "Liken…"

Liken covered her mouth in a passionate kiss. When he raised his head, he began thrusting again. He leaned forward and whispered quietly, tauntingly, between thrusts, "You must not call out. Someone might hear. There may be others here, too. What if they discovered us fucking, *sherree*? How would you feel?"

She moaned and then tried to muffle the sound. He thrust harder, his cock slamming into her now. Still his voice, not quite steady, taunted in her ear, "Are you going to scream for me, *sherree*? When you come will you scream?"

She gritted her teeth as her body tightened. She felt his pleasure grow along with her own. The hard thrust of his length inside her, pumping hard, was pushing her toward release. She craved it. The impulse to cry out was overwhelming. She clamped her mouth shut and tried desperately to be quiet.

Liken felt his breath hitch and tried to suppress his own moan. She was so hot and tight around his aching cock. His words, meant to arouse her, were acting on him, too. He moved his legs forward to gain leverage and thrust harder.

Suddenly, they heard the voice of the clerk from one wall away. "Isshal, is the outfit to your liking?"

Liken never paused in his thrusts. He was not stopping even if the entire planet walked in at that moment. His muscles strained with the strength and depth of his thrusts.

Sharon, on the other hand, was nearly hysterical with arousal and fear. Her heart felt like it would pound right out of her chest. She was right on the edge of release, dying to go over, and terrified of being discovered.

The clerk's voice was closer, rising higher with curiosity. "Isshal, I asked if everything is to your liking?"

Liken growled in a low snarl, "Answer her."

Sharon whispered hoarsely, "Yes," and repeated it more strongly. Liken slammed into her and she turned her face away in a desperate bid for control. Her gaze landed on the hologram couple fucking wildly next to them. Her voice rose into a scream as she yelled, "YES!" Her orgasm exploded through her like the detonation of a bomb.

Liken let out a loud groan as he felt his own scalding release. He felt the pressure move from his spine and then outward as he came in an overwhelming flood of pleasure. He was mindless with the pure animalistic relief of it.

Eventually, his legs grew weak and he shifted, making sure he would not drop her. Dropping his sweaty forehead to Sharon's, he tried to find the strength to move. Sharon was in no better shape. There was a long moment of total silence.

The clerk said with some amusement, "I am glad you are pleased, Isshal. Take as much time with the outfit as you need. I can understand your enthusiasm. I will not bother you again."

They left the store with the new outfit, although Sharon never did try it on at the shop. Liken took care of the payment with his ID card. Sharon never quite looked the clerk in the eye again, although she thought the clerk sent one or two knowing smiles of understanding her way.

Neither Sharon nor Liken could stop smiling. When they were walking home, she found out the Shimerian term for a dressing room was a "trial booth." She had certainly tried something new. Trial booth, indeed.

Coming back to the present with a start, Sharon realized the memory of yesterday was enough to make her wet and aching. She could hear the sounds of Liken taking a shower. She knew she could join him in there, but they were getting ready for a trip to the local Earth library. She really wanted to see it, and Liken had looked so pleased with his little surprise when he announced their destination for today.

Willing her aching body to relax, she focused on how much she had learned this week about Liken and Shimerian culture. It was a strange and beautiful planet, similar to Earth in so many ways and yet so remarkable in its differences. The people she had met were friendly, although seeing so few women and so many men everywhere was startling at times. She had even seen some families with children, although most of the children were boys.

She knew Liken had been careful to shield her from the less pleasant aspects of Shimerian life. Although she had not seen any evidence of it, she knew they had crime because Liken and Tair were cops. A few times on the *shimvehi* she had seen angry-looking faces with exasperated commuter expressions, but there had been no outright violence.

She and Liken had gotten along very well. He was bad about arrogantly assuming he knew what was best for her, but she pointed it out to him quickly enough. There had been minor disagreements, but most of the week had been spent in getting to know each other and learning the little things about each other that only a lover can know.

Liken had discovered that she was scared of heights, secretly read erotic stories, and had incredibly ticklish feet. She had discovered that he loved his job, that he hated Earth television, and that he was a total sucker when it came to small children.

She had been amused to watch as a tiny girl, the daughter of one of his friends, begged him to give her a *delheza* ride. Liken had given her a helpless glance and then proceeded to place the girl on his back, running and hopping while making "*delheza*" noises. He looked ridiculous, but the little girl was laughing wildly.

When Sharon and Liken had left his friends, she had teased him a little about it, but he had merely given her a red-faced shrug, as if to say, "What could I do? She asked me." It was sweet. He could be so sweet.

Sighing, Sharon walked over to the couch and sat down. She could hear the red water turn off in the bathroom. She imagined his naked body emerging from the crimson shower. She was ready to either leave for the library or jump him in the bathroom. She wished he'd hurry up.

Sharon noticed his ID card lying on the couch next to her. Picking it up restlessly, she turned it over and over in her hand. The ID card brought her back to the memory of their shopping trip. Watching him hand over his ID card at the shop that day, Sharon had wondered later about the Shimerian monetary system. Liken explained that all transactions were recorded on his card. Later, he showed her the computer in his home where he transferred the information.

His ID card was similar to a debit card from what she could tell, although it also seemed to be a computer disk of some kind. His computer was linked to central computers maintained by the government. His paycheck was deposited in his account on his computer on certain dates. It was all paperless. The librarian in her admired the organization and efficiency of the system.

Liken appeared in the living room archway, interrupting her thoughts. He looked clean and energized. He was wearing the usual black, but he looked happy and boyishly excited. He really wanted this trip to the library to be a special treat for her. He grinned, looking pleased with himself, and said, "Are you ready, *sherree*? I know you are anxious to leave so I hurried."

Sharon laughed and nodded. She knew what he had been doing. "You know I am. Don't pretend you haven't been lurking in my head."

He laughed with her and corrected, "I do not *lurk, sherree.* I was merely enjoying your memories of our time together."

Crossing the room and extending a hand to her, he grinned shamelessly. "Although perhaps we should squeeze in a quick shopping trip between the library and meeting Tair."

She shook her head in mock reproof. He had been lobbying for another shopping trip since that day. "You have to be the only man in the universe who loves shopping."

Putting her hand in his, she let him pull her up from the couch and felt his arms come around her in a hug. Leaning back to look at his face, she said, "Of course we'll go shopping again." Her face went bright red. "Just not to that same shop."

He threw back his head and laughed. She was such a delightful mix of contradictions-sexy and passionate one moment, and then sweet and shy the next. Leaning down, he whispered into her ear, "As long as we go to a shop with a trial booth."

Sharon could feel heat spread through her at his words. She had been right when she first saw him. He was sex personified. He had only to look at her or say something to her and she melted like wax. She cleared her throat. "I believe we were headed to the library, right?"

Liken was experiencing his own surge of arousal at the thought of another shopping trip. Placing a quick kiss on her forehead and taking his ID card from her hand, he moved away from her and said, "We'd better go. The librarian, Gar, will not be happy if we are late. He is eager to give you a tour."

* * * * *

The library was a wonder. Walking inside the outer archway of the building, Sharon expected to smell the familiar scent of books. Instead, when they walked in, she saw row after row of disks. In the center of the room there were comfortable chairs in a large open space. Seated in the chairs were maybe thirty or so adolescent Shimerian males. They stared at her in apparent fascination until a warning look from Liken made them duck their heads to the notebooks in their hands. Liken took her by the arm and led her to a counter area.

The librarian was a much older male. He had silver hair and an air of quiet dignity. He looked up with a welcoming smile as they approached. Stepping out from behind the counter, he approached Liken.

Handing the man his ID card, Liken nodded his head respectfully and placed a palm on the man's shoulder. The man mirrored his movements, which Sharon knew was the Shimerian form of shaking hands. When they stepped back, Liken put his arm around Sharon and said with obvious pride, "Gar, I would like to introduce you to Sharon Glaston, my pactmate. Sharon, please meet Gar Deyzan'can, the head librarian here and an old friend."

Gar gave Sharon an admiring glance and a warm smile. His voice was strong in contrast to his frail body. "I am most pleased to welcome you, Sharon."

Sharon gave him an answering smile and said, "Thank you. I'm pleased to meet you and very excited to learn about Shimerian libraries."

Liken was quick to add, "Sharon was formerly a librarian on Earth. It is a real pleasure for her to meet her counterpart here." He knew that Gar was aware of that fact, but he wanted to remind him of their earlier conversation.

He was assuming that she would stay here on Shimeria. Sharon didn't appreciate his use of the words "former librarian", but she let it go for the moment. She was really interested in the library and didn't want to spark a disagreement with Liken right now.

Gar seemed to have caught something of the discord in her expression. He said, "It will be a pleasure to show you, Sharon. Let us start your tour." He walked quickly behind the counter and reached down. Pulling a flat notebook from a stack behind his desk, he showed Sharon how to operate the small reader. The entire front of the notebook was a display screen.

Walking over to a row of disks, he placed one in the side of the notebook. He then inserted Liken's ID card into a slot on the other side. With a little hum, the screen lit up and displayed the cover of "A Tale of Two Cities" by Charles Dickens. The words were in English. He handed her the reader.

Placing her finger to the option screen in the upper right hand corner, she learned how to flip from page to page and even how to choose which translation she wanted to read. The language options included Earth languages as well as Shimerian. She learned the disk contained all of Dickens's works, as well as a biography of the author and all literary criticism.

Gar gave a little sigh and told her, "You should have seen the lists of works and other information first, but someone has neglected to press the reset option to return to the main index. It can be frustrating."

Thinking of her own library, she gave him a look of sympathy and said, "I know what you mean. Back at my library, we can never seem to keep people from placing books back on the shelf incorrectly."

Liken saw the look of understanding pass between them and smiled. As Gar led Sharon on a tour of the building, explaining the organization and operation of the library, Liken trailed in their wake. Watching her expressive face, he could see her enthusiasm and love of books. Her curiosity and quiet sincerity charmed Gar just as it did anyone within her orbit. He could tell she was enjoying the outing tremendously. She was happy and he felt a swell of happiness himself that he had given her this experience.

Then, he felt a flash of guilt as he wondered if she knew he had an ulterior motive. He had already spoken with Gar about Sharon working at the library, but had sworn the older man to secrecy. This was, in a way, an informal position interview. Seeing Gar and Sharon in such accord meant she could probably work there on some basis.

It was another step toward convincing her that she could be happy on Shimeria with him. Uneasily wondering if she would accuse him of managing her choices again if she knew, he hoped she would be too happy to examine his motives very closely.

At the end of the tour, Liken and Sharon paused at the main counter. Liken removed his ID card and handed the notebook back to Gar. Placing his hand on the older man's shoulder and nodding his head, he said, "Our thanks for your kind assistance, Gar. We enjoyed the tour very much."

Gar returned the gestures and said with a smile, "No thanks are necessary." He aimed a smiling look Sharon's way. "It is a pleasure to share the experience with a fellow lover of books. She is quite wonderful, Liken. Best get her pledged quickly."

Turning to Sharon, Gar said, "My thanks for your company. I hope I will see you again, Sharon."

Sharon gave him a bright smile. Gar was a knowledgeable and efficient librarian, and a charming man. She said warmly, "Your library is a marvel and I appreciate the tour. I enjoyed it so much. I'm hoping to see you again, too." She wasn't sure if she was staying on Shimeria or not, but now wasn't the time to worry about it.

With smiling faces, Liken and Sharon exited the building and began walking along the pathway outside. Placing her hand on his arm, Sharon looked up at Liken. "Thank you for today."

Looking into her shining eyes, Liken felt a fresh wave of guilt. Deliberately reminding himself that he would have brought her just to experience her enjoyment, he placed a gentle hand against her cheek. "You are welcome, *sherree*. It pleases me to see your happiness."

The look held for a moment as they stared at each other. Removing his hand from her cheek and grabbing hold of hers, he moved them forward. After a few steps, he looked down at her. His eyes held a teasing light. His smile widened into a grin and he wagged his eyebrows suggestively. "If you wish it, you can show me your gratitude later in private."

She laughed and swung their clasped hands as they walked. "Oh, how generous of you. Let's see...what could I possibly do?" She cast him a sideways look under her lashes. "I could cook dinner tonight."

He stopped and with a mock growl, shook his head. "I think you can do better than pushing the meal buttons on our transport machine. I had in mind a more intimate activity." The look he gave her was hot with desire.

She turned her head and made a great production of letting her gaze roam his body. Her expression was speculative. "I don't know...what could be more intimate?"

She appeared to be contemplating the question. Stepping closer and bringing her free hand to his chest, she brushed her body against his. "This could take some thought." She pulled her hand from his grasp and ran it teasingly down his chest to the top of his pants. "A great deal of thought." She could feel his cock start to harden.

He wrapped his arms around her and pulled her into the hard planes of his body. His eyes were dark with desire. "You are an intelligent woman, *sherree*. I have great confidence in you."

Abruptly breaking his hold, she danced away. Her face had flushed with desire as well, but her eyes were teasing.

"Unfortunately, I can't think about it now. We are late for supper with Tair."

His look said she could expect retribution later. "Yes, teasing does tend to make one forget the time." He was secretly thrilled with her easy flirtation. She felt comfortable enough to tease him sexually.

With a mock sigh and a glance at the time device on his wrist, he said, "We will continue this later. Now, I am sorry to say, you are right. We will be late if we do not hurry."

With matching smiles, they hurried along the pathways leading to the eatery where Tair waited. When they entered the building where they had met him the last time, Sharon barely noticed the sudden hush and the fascinated stares. Looking around for Tair, she spotted him in the far right corner of the room. Smiling and waving, she headed for his table.

Weaving her way there with Liken behind her, she never saw Tair's sweeping look around the room. His predatory gaze froze his fellow diners in place until they looked quickly away from Sharon's form and focused on eating. The mental warning had been so brief and effective that Sharon reached the table completely unaware.

With a silent nod of acknowledgement for his assistance, Liken sank into a chair next to Sharon. In contrast to just a few seconds earlier, Tair's face had a gentle smile when he turned to Sharon. "You are looking quite beautiful, Sharon."

Smiling with obvious happiness, Sharon said. "Thank you, Tair. We went to the library today."

Tair frowned in mock astonishment. "So that is what has left you flushed and put a glow in your eyes?" He glanced over at Liken and shook his head in reproof. "We need to have a discussion, brother. "

Watching the blush climb into Sharon's cheeks, Liken said with a laugh. "I do not believe the library is solely responsible, Tair." He leaned toward her and gently nuzzled her cheek.

"Sharon has found other things on Shimeria that are also highly enjoyable."

Sharon felt like her face was on fire. They were ganging up on her. She was in too good a mood to let them get to her. She felt sexy and happy and powerful. She was not going to give in to embarrassment at their teasing.

Clearing her throat, she decided to fight fire with fire. Placing her hand on Liken's thigh under the table, she watched his teasing grin begin to fade. She gently stroked the taut muscles in his thigh, her fingers heading up toward his crotch. Liken had turned to stone at the first touch of her hand.

Turning toward Tair, she leaned toward him and spoke in a throaty voice that spelled pure sex. "Oh, yes. I have found several activities to...arouse my...interests."

Tair seemed trapped in her heated gaze, his heart rate climbing at the sound of her husky voice. Deliberately moistening her lips, she smiled inwardly as both men stared in fascination. This femme fatale business was easier than she thought it would be.

Carefully straightening her shoulders as she leaned back in her chair, her breasts rose to prominent attention. Again, both men seemed unable to pull their gaze away. Feeling the power of her allure, she smiled and raised her free hand to lightly stroke her throat. "Are you guys really hot?" Her mind filled with naughty images, the fantasies making her pupils dilate.

Their eyes widened. Tair stared at her stroking hand and then dropped his eyes to her breasts. Her nipples hardened. Wetting his lips, he swallowed.

Liken was in no better shape. Her hand under the table reached its destination. His bulging arousal was pushing against his pants, flexing under her fingers. He made a strangled sound and quickly moved one hand to hold her in place. He was rock hard and throbbing.

In an innocent voice she exclaimed, "I think it's hot in here, don't you?" Deciding she had neatly turned the tables on them

Marly Chance

both, she looked around for a waiter. Catching his eye, she nodded toward their table. He walked toward them quickly.

The waiter gave her an efficient smile and asked, "How can I be of assistance? Have you decided on your choices?" His words forced their attention away from her.

Liken's grip on her hand relaxed and she took advantage of the moment to pull her hand back into her own lap. Tair sat back in his chair and visibly worked to regain his composure. She looked from one man to the other. Other than the dark awareness in their eyes, they looked pretty normal.

In a cool and natural voice, she said, "I think they could use something to cool off. What kind of refreshing beverage would you recommend?"

As she discussed the various choices with the waiter, Liken and Tair looked at each other. Tair's eyes were speculative as he spoke in their own language. "*That one is deceptive. She has more fire than she knows.*" He was still sweating a little from his reaction to her.

Liken's eyes were gleaming. Sharon was far bolder and passionate than most people realized, including herself. "*Yes, I know. She is incredible.*"

Tair shook his head in disbelief. "A librarian. I thought she was the quiet one."

Liken laughed quietly. "She sees herself that way. To be fair, I don't think she realized she was broadcasting her fantasies to the two of us. She is unaware of our link or the power of such images."

"*You haven't told her of linking? Or what it means?*" Tair was incredulous. He was shocked that Sharon was unaware of the coming link. It was natural to hide the knowledge from prospective Earth mates until after the pact to lesson any fear, but he could not believe Liken had not explained to Sharon about it before now.

Liken was exasperated. "I am only just now getting her comfortable with merging, brother. She was sexually

- 112 -

inexperienced. I'm not going to scare her to death." Sharon had been resistant to intimacy from the start. He had no doubt that she would react badly to the idea of linking. Human culture was so strange.

Tair conceded that point. "I can understand. You don't have much time left, though. We must perform the linking tomorrow next. Shocking her at the last minute is not a good idea."

Liken grimaced. "I know. I plan to tell her tonight. I thought after an enjoyable day and some time in your company, she might not be as shocked at the idea. You could play your part by staying non-threatening and charming." It was more of a reminder than a request.

Sharon spoke up at that moment, startling the two men. "Hey, guys, I hate to break up your little talk, but the waiter here needs to know what you want." She was curious about why they were speaking Shimerian suddenly.

When they turned identical charming smiles in her direction, she felt distinctly uneasy. What were they hiding? Although she had picked up a few Shimerian words and phrases, she had no idea what they had been saying. If she stayed on this planet, she would need to learn the language. Being in the dark about what they had been discussing was making her nervous.

When they each had given the waiter their choices for the meal, the waiter left for a back room. Silence fell between them. Liken and Tair could both sense her rising uneasiness. Hitting on something that would divert her attention and make her happy, Tair spoke quickly. "Sharon, I have good news for you."

His comment startled her. She couldn't imagine what he meant. "Good news for me?"

"Yes, I think it will make you very happy." With a glance toward Liken, he turned to face her fully. "Kate is my pactmate."

Her shock was easy to see. "What?!"

"I will be invoking the Oath after you return to take your pledge next week. You and Kate will not be separated." He waited for her look of happiness and relief. He had looked forward to seeing her reaction to this news for some time.

She began laughing, which caught the two men by surprise. As her laughter rose in volume and her shoulders began to shake, their puzzlement grew.

Tair, wondering if he should take insult, could make no sense of her reaction. "You find the thought amusing?"

"I find the thought hysterical," she choked out. "She's gonna kick your ass."

He looked thunderous in response.

Liken quickly cut in, "I am sure Sharon does not mean to insult you, brother." He shot a reprimanding look at Sharon.

She just rolled her eyes in response. She really hadn't meant to insult him. The comment wasn't directed at Tair's abilities as much as it was Kate's reaction. Bringing her laughter under control, she tried for a conciliatory tone. "I didn't mean to insult you, Tair. Really. No offense meant."

Tair's voice was stiff. "You do not know me very well, Sharon."

Sharon realized he was serious. He felt insulted, his pride injured. Feeling badly, she tried to explain, "No, I know that. I don't doubt you or your, uh, abilities. I have to point out, though, that I do know Kate. She's my best friend in the world so I can tell you the truth. Nobody walks on Kate. She can be a cast iron bitch if you try."

Tair's shoulders relaxed a little. "I know about her temper, Sharon." That temper was going to make things quite interesting between them. He smiled at the thought.

She leaned forward. "That's not really what I meant. Kate doesn't do submissive. Liken's domineering ways make me crazy and, believe me, I let him know about it. Kate, on the other hand, would've just killed him and been done with it. No need to compromise or explain. She might even be a little sorry afterward, but she'd get the job done. She'd never put up with Shimerian attitudes." She looked at Liken to see if he, at least, understood.

"Sharon, look at me." It was an order, given by Tair in a voice that was intense and compelling. He didn't sound like himself. She watched as Tair's face grew harsh. His eyes, which had looked gentle and charming in the past, took on a predatory hardness. His mouth held a touch of cruelty. "Do I look like I do not know how to get what I want?" The change in him was drastic to see.

"Tair?" Sharon said his name with a questioning note. She felt a pang of pure panic. The man sitting next to her had become a dangerous stranger. He stared at her in silence. She swallowed. "I get your point." She clasped her hands together in her lap and suddenly wondered if insulting him had been such a bright idea.

Liken's hand covered hers in her lap with a comforting warmth. Aiming a warning glance at Tair, he said, "My brother will make Kate very happy in the end, *sherree*. Do not worry."

Sharon wouldn't place any bets on that statement. She was relieved to see the waiter approaching the table. As he placed their dishes in front of each of them, they remained silent.

Even after he left, Sharon stayed silent, lost in her thoughts. She had no idea if she was staying on Shimeria, regardless of how well things had been going. The last week had been a kind of honeymoon period, but she knew there were bound to be conflicts ahead. She and Liken had spent most of their time in a sensual haze, not wanting anything to spoil the pleasure. They were both on their best behavior. It couldn't last indefinitely.

She wasn't sure if she would stay, so the thought of Kate becoming Tair's pactmate didn't bring a lot of comfort. If she stayed, Kate might still file incompatible. If Sharon filed incompatible, Kate might choose to stay. It was unlikely, but seeing Tair in a new light, she knew it was possible. Kate was used to calling all the shots with men. Sharon had always figured the right man for Kate would be one she couldn't walk all over. Maybe Tair was the right man. Or alien, in this case. Either way, the future was still uncertain.

"You are not eating, Sharon." Liken's voice broke into her thoughts. "Are you truly upset by Tair's news?"

Liken knew by her face that she was upset. He was trying to stay out of her thoughts more, since they were both adjusting to the intimacy. He knew it made her uncomfortable, particularly when she was upset.

Sharon made an effort to appear more relaxed. She took a quick bite of her food, but her turmoil made it tasteless. "Not at all. I'm fine." Her deadpan voice said just the opposite.

Tair felt guilty for ruining her mood. She had been radiant when she entered the eatery and sat down at the table. His voice held unmistakable remorse when he spoke. "I thought only to bring you happiness with my news. My apology to you, Sharon."

She looked into a face that had grown softer. His eyes sought to reassure her. She liked Tair, even trusted him to some degree because he was Liken's brother. He was trying to regain her earlier comfort with him. She wasn't fooled.

With serious eyes, she studied him. "Thank you, Tair, but the apology isn't necessary. What happens between you and Kate will be up to the two of you. I would like you both to be happy. If you end up happy together, that would be terrific."

She wanted to put them on an easier footing as well. With more enthusiasm than she felt, she picked up another square-shaped bite of mystery meat and popped it in her mouth. In an abrupt change of subject, she swallowed and said, "What exactly am I eating again? This is delicious." She picked up another bite and turned to Liken to answer her question.

He regarded her solemnly. "I am glad you find it so tasty, *sherree*. It is called *ufrantri* and is considered quite a delicacy."

He waited as she put the bite in her mouth and began to chew. "The literal translation would be yellow worm in your language I believe." Sharon choked a little as his words registered. Liken winked at Tair.

Worm? They were feeding her worm?! Sharon felt the moist meat in her mouth and nearly gagged. Should she swallow it or find some way to ditch it in her napkin? She was pretty sure it was bad table manners to throw up the main dish in a crowded restaurant. Even on weird Shimeria. She decided then and there that adventure sucked. Exotic cuisine. Yeah. Right.

Liken did not let her suffer for long. "Go ahead and swallow it, *sherree*. It is not really a worm. I said that was the literal translation. It is actually not a meat at all, but a tubular vegetable." He could not contain his laugh at the killing look she aimed his way.

Tair began laughing, too. "It is similar to your potato, Sharon, but longer in length and narrower." As she swallowed and continued to glare at both of them, they laughed harder.

Liken's voice was apologetic but his eyes sparkled with mirth. "I could not resist."

Reaching down, he picked up another square shaped bite. This one was brown. Holding it out to her, he said. "Come, *sherree*, where is your sense of adventure? I would not feed you something abhorrent, would I?"

Taking the brown thing in her hand, she examined it suspiciously. Her voice was dry. She said firmly, "I believe I prefer my adventure between the covers of a book."

"Not you, *sherree*. You are a woman of fire." His voice held a sultry warmth while his eyes dared her to put the bite in her mouth.

Sharon felt the heat climbing into her cheeks at his passionate reference. He was driving her crazy on purpose. She was sure of it.

"Oh, that's right. I'm a new woman these days. I think nothing of interplanetary travel. I seek out new life and new civilizations. I boldly go where..." She slapped her free hand against her forehead in mock surprise. "Whoops, that's not me. What was I thinking? I'm just the idiot who tastes whatever you give her."

She rolled her eyes. Pushing aside any thoughts on what it might be, she put the bite in her mouth. She was relieved to find it tasted pretty good.

Liken watched her with satisfaction. "An idiot? I think not. I would say you trust me, *sherree*. And that makes you very smart indeed."

"I trust you not to poison me at least, "she said with an exasperated smile. Her voice was light. She wasn't about to feed that colossal arrogance of his.

His gaze held hers. "Progress is still progress, however small." Both had forgotten Tair, who was listening to the exchange with great interest.

She shrugged and looked away. "Or maybe I just can't resist a dare."

She felt him lean toward her. His breath tickled her ear as he whispered, "We shall see, *sherree*. Soon. In that you can trust." To Sharon, the words sounded part promise, part threat. With Liken, it never paid to grow too complacent.

The rest of the meal went by uneventfully. They talked and laughed, enjoying themselves. When Liken and Sharon left the restaurant, she felt alive and happy in a way she couldn't remember. Pushing all thoughts of the coming decision from her mind, she basked in her newfound contentment with Liken. They made love that evening with tenderness and passion, both of them avoiding anything that might break their fragile sense of happiness and accord.

That profound sense of harmony made what happened next seem even more painful. Everything went straight to hell the next day. After a lovely evening with Liken and Tair and then a night of incredible pleasure in Liken's arms, Sharon had no clue the very next day that things were going to change in a heartbeat.

Or rather, things were going to change with one word.

Chapter Nine

"You want me to do *what* with your brother tomorrow?" Her voice was strangled with disbelief.

They were sitting in the living room after supper or "evemeal" as he called it. They were casually talking and the conversation had drifted to Tair. Leaning cozily against his side, listening to the mellow sounds drifting from the machine hidden in the wall to her right, Sharon had no clue he was about to toss a conversational grenade her way. She moved out of his arms and turned around to look at him.

He knew he looked like he was headed for a funeral. He had been dreading this conversation for so long. He winced and said, "I will explain…"

"Explain?" she interrupted. "Yeah, that would be good. Because I could have sworn you just told me I'm supposed to get it on with your brother!" Her voice was rising. Surely he hadn't meant what she thought he meant.

He looked confused. He was familiar with most human slang, but her words made no sense. "I'm not sure of your meaning."

"Let me clarify then. Did you just tell me that you're going to try to force me to have sex with Tair?" Her gaze locked on his face, hoping for some sign of disagreement.

His expression cleared. He looked appalled. "That is not what I said." Slowly enunciating his words, he said, "You will be linking with my brother."

Now it was her turn to look confused. "I don't understand."

Liken took a deep breath as he gathered his patience for the battle ahead. He should have told her last night as he had planned, but he had procrastinated, not wanting to disrupt their harmony. He could no longer wait.

"These are dangerous times, Sharon. Believe me, I see that as a guardian every day. I have protected you from harm so far, but I will not always be with you. You are linked with me through our merging, but Shimerian law and custom require at least one other link. If you were in distress, I would know it and come to your aid. The second link with a close friend or family member is to ensure that someone else is available as well."

She cautiously nodded her head. "I can understand the theory, but I'm not merging with Tair."

His eyes went hard. "No, you will not *merge* with Tair."

"What do you mean by linking then?" She was calming down. He wasn't talking about her having sex with Tair. Maybe this wasn't as bad as she thought.

"He will link to you mentally. Think of it as a pathway from your mind to his."

"You mean he'll be in my head, too?" She was not having two guys traipsing around her thoughts whenever they wanted. Liken was bad enough.

"Not really, *sherree*. His mind will pierce the shield I have built for you and leave an opening for him like a doorway." His voice was reassuring. He was glad to see her calming.

She didn't really like the idea of a doorway in her head. "Can anybody walk in?"

"No, only Tair and, of course, me."

She mulled it over. "Can he walk in anytime he wants and just know what I'm thinking?"

Again, he answered in that reasonable tone. "He would only travel the link if you were in distress, *sherree*. Tair is trustworthy. He will not spy on your private thoughts. He will hear when you broadcast loudly, but otherwise your thoughts are safe." They would be even safer when he taught her to broadcast less openly, but the process would take time.

She couldn't shake her unease. She liked Tair. She could even understand having a second hotline installed as a backup for emergencies. She didn't like the thought of giving anyone access to her mind. She didn't have any choice with Liken. It was too late. They were already merged. Linking with Tair, however, was still within her power to choose. Another thought occurred. "Why did you say tomorrow? Were you just suggesting we get it over with then?"

Liken's mouth firmed. "Tomorrow is the tenth day of our knowing period. Merging and linking must be complete by the end of that day. It is the law."

She looked indignant. "Screw the law."

He felt his temper begin to stir, but held it back. "Again, it is there for your protection, Sharon. Females on this planet are cherished and protected above all else."

"From what? This place is peaceful. It's not exactly a hotbed of crime. I don't understand what I'm supposed to be protected against!" She was trying to sort through the confusion.

In a careful voice he told her. "When we merged, I built a shield to protect you. It is not invincible. But when Tair layers his strength over mine, you will be safe from nearly anyone. There is evil on this planet, just as evil exists on your own. The difference is that on my planet, an evil man can use his mind to cause harm. He can literally probe into the minds of others. If they fight him, he can cause a great deal of damage. When I probe someone who is unwilling, I do it with great skill and care. I do not cause harm. I care whether I hurt or kill someone."

His mouth was grim. "You cannot even imagine what occurs when a criminal attempts a merge on an unwilling female. She will fight him because it is instinctive. When I merged with you, as a human you had absolutely no defenses.

You were not able to struggle and I was careful to cause no damage. Now that I have put defenses in place for you by building a shield, for someone to try to force a merge…"

His voice trailed off as if he didn't even want to contemplate it. "It would take a lot to break my shielding. If it broke, you might survive, but the damage would be terrible. By adding Tair's shielding to mine, we increase the odds that it would never happen."

He paused, drew a deep breath, and continued. "I would see you protected to the greatest degree possible. Adding Tair's shielding to mine is necessary, *sherree*."

Sharon nodded her head in understanding, but she wasn't completely sure that it was really necessary. This mental shielding business was bizarre.

To make sure she understood his point, he gave her an example. "What if I put a piece of cloth over a peach? I could take a needle and it would take only a pinprick through the cloth to get to the peach."

Holding her gaze, he willed her to take his next words seriously. "Now what if I take a metal bowl and place it over that same peach? It would take a sharp hammer and considerable force to punch through the metal. But if the hammer punched through, you know what would happen to the peach."

She looked sick. "I see what you mean." There was no missing that imagery. "So between you and Tair, nobody's gonna get through."

He hoped she was right. "There are no guarantees, *sherree*. Tair and I are both very strong shielders. It would be nearly impossible. I cannot lie and tell you it could not happen. I can only say that we would probably all three die in such a case."

His words struck right into her heart. He would protect her with his life. Tair would protect her with his life. Her chest tightened with the thought. In a desperate attempt to lighten the moment, she blurted out, "Who says guys can't commit?"

He let out a startled laugh. For a moment there, he had been mortally afraid she was going to cry or something equally as terrifying. With tremendous relief, he said, "Indeed, we poor males are often judged most unfairly." He winked.

She laughed too. Regaining her composure, she became serious again. "All right, I'll link with Tair. What exactly do we need to do tomorrow?"

He was past the first obstacle but he knew her agreement was not secure. Bracing himself for the explosion, he said calmly, "At the point of your orgasm, while we are merged, he will link with you." He waited in silence for her to work it out.

Her brow wrinkled in confusion. "That's bizarre. Why the point of orgasm?" She still hadn't considered the rest of his statement.

"At the point of orgasm, *sherree*, you are most vulnerable. You are out of control, unable to think. Your senses and the power of our minds merging will overwhelm you. There is no chance you will try to fight him."

"Couldn't he just link with me in my sleep?" she suggested hopefully. It seemed more logical and less bizarre.

"I cannot merge with you when you are sleeping without sleeping myself. Tair will need my help to get past my shielding. Besides, you might awaken and try to fight him." The tension of waiting was killing him.

"But how will he know the exact point of orgasm?" A sudden thought crossed her mind but she couldn't believe it.

Very calmly, speaking softly, Liken said. "Because he will be with us."

Her eyes widened and she shook her head in automatic denial. "With us?!" Her heart began pounded and she felt lightheaded. "What do you mean with us?!"

"He will be in the room with us. Once I have merged with you, he will be touching you. He will wait and then link with you when you come." His voice was firm. The expected explosion occurred immediately.

"*No way*! I can't believe this! I can't believe you would even go along with this!" Her voice began to get shrill. "One minute you tell me you and Tair would die trying to protect me. The next minute you casually announce that the three of us…"

Her voice broke and tears were a burning pressure behind her eyes. She jumped up from the couch and turned her back on him. Staring at the wall, she tried to regain some control.

Liken felt his chest tighten at the anguish in her voice. He opened his mouth to speak, but she seemed to sense it and held her hand up. It was as if by throwing her hand up, she could ward off his words.

He sucked in a breath and let it out slowly. He couldn't handle the thought of reducing her to tears. He waited for her to speak.

After a minute, her shoulders straightened and she turned to face him again. Her eyes were dry chips of ice, but her voice was even colder. "I'm not fucking your brother." Each word was spaced with emphasis.

The welling emotion in Liken's chest turned to fury in an instant. "I did not ask you to fuck my brother."

Her voice was like a bullet. "Then what do you mean he'll be there during sex. How will he be touching me?" Crushing cynicism filled her tone.

His voice was harsh. "Most of the time he will be across the room. After I merge with you, he will press his body along yours."

"*No*. I won't be any part of this." She spoke resolutely. "I'll take my chances. No link." She started pacing, her movements echoing her inner agitation.

Liken stood up and towered over her, stopping her in mid-stride. Any last bit of patience he had was gone. "You will do it. Tair will build you a better shield."

"He can build a better mousetrap if he wants to," she shot back, "but he's not doing it in my head."

He grabbed her arms and glared down at her. "There will be no sex between you since that is your will. But body contact is necessary." He felt like shaking her, but didn't.

She raised a rebellious face upward. "Oh right." Her voice was sharp enough to cut glass. "He'll just be watching us and rubbing against me while we fuck. I don't know why I thought that was sexual."

His jaw was so tight it would probably lock permanently. "Enough. You will do as you are told." His tone was final.

She gave a laugh of disbelief. "That's it? I'll do as I'm told?!" She thought that maybe her head would blow off from sheer temper. "Listen, big guy, you merged with the wrong gal. I'm not a child you can order around."

His voice was ruthless. "You will obey me in this. It is for your protection."

The tension was thick enough to cut with a knife. "I won't obey you in anything, but especially not this. What are you going to do tomorrow, rape me?" Her voice turned ugly. "Will Tair watch that too?"

He abruptly turned loose of her. His voice was colder than she'd ever heard it. "I am done with this. I will be back later when you have regained your reason."

He turned and headed for the door. Hitting the button nearly hard enough to leave an impression in the wall, he strode past the sliding door and turned back. His voice was mocking. "Your trust is quite touching, Sharon. Your resourcefulness is impressive as well. You have found yet another way to run."

He leaned wearily against the doorway. Bitterness was carved into his face. "You forget—I know your fantasies. I was at the table with Tair last night when certain images ran through your mind. You grew wet at the thought. Deny it to me if you must, but be honest with yourself. The thought of my brother in the room with us scares you, but you are not as outraged as you pretend."

He stared at her for a minute, but she made no response. He turned and walked down the pathway. The door slid shut in his wake.

His words struck her like a blow. Sinking to the ground, she tried to calm down. As she wrapped her arms around herself in unconscious comfort, she felt numb with grief. Hurt was a living thing in her chest.

He didn't love her. You couldn't have love without respect. He thought she would obey him like a child. She could only gasp in outrage. He thought it was okay for Tair to be with them.

It was at that moment she realized she could feel his hurt and anger pressing upon hers. It was flowing between them, a benefit of merging, causing magnified grief. Wiping a hand across her face wearily, she wondered how things could have gone so wrong so fast.

Cosmic Destiny. It sucked.

Chapter Ten

Tair opened the door of his home to find a seething Liken on his doorstep. He spoke in Shimerian. *"Enter, brother. I could feel your anger raging at me all the way from your dwelling."*

Liken walked past him and Tair pushed the button, sliding the door into place. Turning around, he leaned against it and watched his brother storm into the living room. Walking to a button on the wall, Liken pressed it and removed a bottle of *lerj*. Bringing it to his mouth, he took a healthy swallow.

Tair winced. The potency of the alcoholic drink was well known. He could attest to it himself. Liken must have scorched his insides with that big of a swallow.

Moving to join his brother in the living room, he sat down on the couch. Liken paced with the bottle still in his hand. In the voice of someone trying to sooth a wild animal, Tair said, *"Liken, you and Sharon are both broadcasting at an alarming level. "* He rubbed his hand across his aching forehead.

Liken really looked at his brother for the first time. There were lines of stress in Tair's face and there was dull pain in his eyes. Knowing his own face looked worse, he felt guilty nonetheless. *"My apologies, Tair."* He made a visible effort to calm down.

"You and Sharon are building the hurt and anger between you, Liken. You need to pull back from her for a time. It is dangerous. "Tair hated to see his brother in such shape. The voice of reason was definitely needed here.

With a nod of assent, Liken worked on withdrawing and blocking Sharon as much as he could. He could not sever himself from her completely but he could block her out for a time. They both needed it. He knew Tair was right.

Tair gave him a tired smile of approval. "I am glad you see reason. You need to put your emotions aside, brother, and begin thinking instead."

Liken felt another wave of anger move through him, but he focused on getting it under control. *"I suppose you know what was said."*

Tair's voice was wry. *"I could not help knowing. It was practically an assault."* He felt sorry for both of them. The angry words and feelings from their argument made him feel raw and unhappy.

Liken felt guilty again. "We had no right to so abuse you, Tair. I can only say that we are newly merged and we will learn better control with time. Again, my apologies."

Tair waived them aside. *"There is no need, Liken. I am much more concerned with what has happened. Why is she so resistant?"* He couldn't understand why Sharon would be so against such a natural thing.

Liken knew Sharon very well, perhaps even better than she knew herself. "There are many reasons. She is afraid, uncomfortable with her growing sexuality. She doesn't completely trust me. She was raised in a culture very different from our own. She viewed you being in the room as a desire on my part to share her. It doesn't reconcile with her idea of love."

Tair shook his head. "Those are all things that can be handled with reassurances and patience. We are a very sexual culture, but possessive as well. You need to get her to understand that my linking with her is not a betrayal. It is customary. As a matter of fact, it is necessary. She judges it as an infidelity and assumes you do not care for her. You must show her she is wrong."

Liken collapsed into the chair across from Tair and took another swig from the bottle. "Easily said, brother. How can I make her understand? I tried reasoning, I tried ordering, and still she refuses to trust me. She pulls back from me."

He slouched down and laid his head on the back of the chair. "She fights me for every inch of progress. I think I can hold her and then she slides out of my arms and runs from me again. It is maddening."

"*So it is just your pride aching.*" Tair's voice was suspiciously smooth.

"*Of course.*" Liken's voice was firm, but he was rubbing his hand over his chest unconsciously. "*She is merely a woman, pactmate or no. I grow sick of rejection.*"

Nodding in agreement, Tair gave him a half smile. "So do not worry, brother. In a few days, you can file incompatible. You will never see her again. The portal to Earth is always open. There are many females there besides her. Not another pactmate for you like her, but there will be females who are not so impossible."

Liken's head came up. He heard the goading tone in his brother's voice but ignored it. His voice rose as he agreed, "*That is right! I do not need this chaos. Who needs her?*"

Tair sat waiting silently. It wouldn't be long, he was sure. The room was quiet until the silence was broken by Liken's sigh. His voice full of misery, Liken said, "*I do. She is mine and I am not giving her up.*"

Tair sat forward and grinned. "Okay, brother. Then you will keep her." His face turned serious as he said, "What you have tried has not worked. It is time to stop trying and start doing. You have never backed down from a challenge before."

Liken set the bottle down and leaned forward with new resolution. "You are right. Tonight she is through running from me. What cannot be taken with gentle patience can still be held by force."

He felt a new sense of calm and purpose. Sharon was at home weeping in anguish, he was sure. He would go to her and make things right. Then, he would force her to face herself and her relationship with him.

Opening his block with her, Liken went completely still. Both men felt the blood in their veins turn to ice. Jumping to their feet, they headed in a panic for the front door.

Sharon was not at home. And she certainly wasn't crying.

Chapter Eleven

Sharon was at the eatery. She had grown tired of sitting on the living room floor after Liken left. After about a half-hour in absolute misery she felt a sudden emptiness. Without being sure how she knew, she could tell Liken had withdrawn from her nearly completely. She should have been happy to have him out of her head. Instead, she felt a sense of loneliness that only added to her hurt.

Finally, she stood up with renewed purpose. With each step around the room, her hurt became swallowed by anger. How dare he order her around and expect her to wait for his return like a child? She was a grown woman. She had come to this planet, had mind-blowing sex with a near stranger, gotten laid in a dressing room, and eaten exotic food. She wasn't some sweet helpless young thing too scared to leave the house.

She was tired of just reacting to whatever he did next. It was time to take charge. Past time. He had hurt her, but she wasn't going to sit around and whine about it. The thought of possible danger crossed her mind. She was connected to the big idiot if she ran into mind trouble. Anything else she could handle herself. She needed to get away from *his* house. She was going out. To hell with him.

Leaving the house, she walked angrily for a while, not really caring of the direction. She was oblivious to her glittering skin or the beautiful glow of the buildings in the silvery moonlight. She didn't see anyone else until she was nearly in front of the eatery.

There were Shimerian males coming out and a few going in. Their dark features reminded her of Liken and she moved forward with resolution. She was not a prisoner, waiting for her jailer to give her permission to leave the house and have a night out.

Walking through the archway, she searched the room until she spotted an empty table. Around her, a dozen Shimerian men paused with their drinks halfway to their mouths. Another handful nearly choked as they watched her cross the room. There was complete silence.

Sharon was angry enough not to care. Sitting down at the empty table, she sent a sweeping glare around the room. Just great. More men. Like she wasn't sick to death of them already. And where were the damn women on this planet tonight? It was testosterone hell.

A waiter she recognized from her previous visits appeared at the table after nearly running across the room. She looked up at him with a grim parody of a smile. "Bring me something alcoholic and put it on that idiot Liken's account. You remember me, don't you?"

He flashed her a cautious smile. "Of course, Isshal." He seemed ruffled. "But I don't understand…alcoholic?" The word was unfamiliar but his shock at seeing a lone unescorted female in the eatery at this hour was enough to cause greater confusion

She searched for another word to explain. "Fermented. You know, a beer. Hell, a shot of tequila might be better."

He must have understood what she meant because he nodded and hurried into the back. Sharon glanced around the room again, noticing conversations in low tones being carried on around the room. At least they weren't staring at her like an exotic animal escaped from the zoo anymore.

Her thoughts turned inward as she thought about the ugly scene with Liken. The more she tried to push it away, the more their angry words echoed in her head. She was trying to stay angry. Angry was a lot better than hurt.

The waiter came back with a small bowl and set it down in front of her. She looked down at it in surprise. It looked like cream of wheat or something. She couldn't believe it. She was too shocked to say anything as he nodded and scurried away.

She felt defeated. Her shoulders slumped. Nothing on this planet made any sense. She muttered to herself, "Ask for a beer and they bring me baby cereal. I hate this place. I feel like an idiot. What am I saying? Men are idiots."

She felt a big body drop gracefully into the chair across from her. Lifting her gaze from the bowl, her mouth dropped open in shock. In the chair across from her sat possibly the most gorgeous guy she'd ever seen. He had a face like a dark angel. His black hair fell in soft waves just ending at the top of massive shoulders. He could have dropped down from heaven if it weren't for his eyes. They were dark brown, nearly black and the hardness in them said he'd seen hell.

His lips curved upward in a smile that never reached those eyes. "Even idiots have their uses, *sherree*, wouldn't you agree?"

The sound of him calling her by the same endearment Liken used caused her heart to clutch. "What does *sherree* mean?" Yet another question she should have asked long ago.

He looked amused by her question. He spoke in English with just a touch of an accent. "It is an endearment that doesn't really translate well. I guess the closest English word would be baby."

Anger washed through her all the way down to her toes. "It figures. He treats me like a child. I should have guessed he's been calling me one."

His smile widened. His voice was like chocolate, soothing and wickedly tempting at the same time. "I cannot imagine any man treating you like a child."

She blushed. She stammered out a reply as her heart beat against her ribs. "I didn't mean…" There wasn't anything to say that wouldn't mortify her even worse.

He was openly grinning now and it transformed his face. He looked like a mischievous little boy. "I presume you are speaking of your missing pactmate?"

She was startled. "Why would you assume I have a pactmate? And why would you assume he's missing? I could just be out on the town by myself to relax after a hard day at the office. Besides, I could be pledged."

He shook his head. "You are unescorted. You are too beautiful to be unclaimed. And you are from Earth. Yet, you are still here alone. That means there is an unhappy pactmate somewhere close by." His voice was persuasive. "Tell me his name. Perhaps I will not mind fighting him for a woman such as you."

That scared her a little. She wasn't the type of woman that men brawled over. She wouldn't mind kicking Liken's ass, but she didn't want him actually fighting some other guy. Especially not someone like this guy. They would hurt each other for sure.

She needed to get rid of him. With a little shrug, she said, "Does it matter? Look, I just came here for a beer. I've got one idiot male and I don't really need another one, okay?" Sharon looked away, hoping he would take the hint and leave her alone.

His voice was firm. "What is your name? And his? I will not leave until I know." Turning and staring into those dark eyes, she knew he wasn't going to let the matter drop. And he wasn't going to leave either.

"I'm Sharon Glaston. My pactmate is Liken da'Kamon." Just saying Liken's name made her eyes burn and her chest tighten. Suddenly, she felt despondent again. She looked away or she would have seen his obvious surprise.

When she had a little more control, she turned to face him and saw him eyeing her speculatively. His grin was back. "So, Liken is the idiot causing you such distress."

Her eyebrows rose. "You know him?"

He said easily, "We have met. What has he done to make you so unhappy, Sharon?"

She wasn't sure she wanted to tell him. He seemed nice, but there were those hard eyes.

He saw her indecision. With a nod, he gestured the waiter over. Speaking in Shimerian, he had a conversation with the waiter, who then went to the back. Focusing on Sharon again, he flashed her a friendly, easygoing smile. "I am Jadik Listan'dy. I will buy you that beer."

She smiled because she couldn't help it. "That would be great. Thanks, Jadik." For the next half-hour, they kept up a friendly conversation. Sharon was on her second beer at that point, so she was feeling much more relaxed. Jadik seemed a lot less dangerous now. His light question caught her by surprise. "Are you linked with Tair?"

He said it so naturally that she answered without thought. "No and I'm not going to. He can go to hell." Her voice changed from friendly to angry as thoughts of her earlier conversation with Liken came to mind.

His eyebrows lifted. "I would have thought... They are brothers, after all. Who has Liken picked then?" He seemed genuinely surprised.

Sharon smiled grimly and said, "Oh, he picked Tair all right. But it's not going to happen."

Jadik stared at her a minute. Finally he asked in a neutral voice, "You object to Tair?"

She gave an exasperated sigh. "No, I like Tair just fine. That doesn't mean I want to link with him." How could she make yet another male understand that she didn't want to link with anyone?

His face turned serious. "You must link with someone, Sharon. It is for your own protection." He paused, then continued, "And it is the law."

Sharon's expression closed up. "I don't need this lecture from you, too."

Jadik studied her curiously for a minute like he couldn't figure her out. "Why would you object to linking?"

Her face turned red. "Look, it may be normal on this planet, but I'm not *from* here, okay? I don't do threesomes." His brows climbed higher. She mumbled a little and then finished with, "Hey, I'm a librarian," as if that explained everything.

Jadik laughed. He was really enjoying her. Too bad Liken was her match. "Sharon, I think what you have here is a cultural misunderstanding."

He sobered. "Linking must be done at orgasm, there is no other way. The participants must be touching. The more contact the better. Again, there is no other way. But, it is perfectly natural. There will be touching, but it will go only as far as the three parties decide."

She flashed him a skeptical look. "And how far is that?"

He grinned. "That will be up to the three of you. Whatever happens, I cannot see you doing something you do not want. Not the woman who burst through the door into this place and demanded a drink. I would say you will be fine."

She flushed and looked uneasy. "I don't know. I don't like the idea of it."

He leaned forward and his grin grew even broader. "Don't you?"

Her face was on fire. She shook her head in denial. He laughed softly and reached across the table to catch her hand. Rubbing his thumb gently across her palm, he said softly, "Maybe I should ask Liken to let me substitute for Tair."

Her gaze flew to his face in panic. He was only kidding, she was pretty sure. Her pulse was pounding so hard he could probably feel it. "I don't think that's a good idea." She pulled on her hand, but he didn't release it.

"Why don't I ask them both? They should be here any moment now." As he said the last word, Liken and Tair came through the front door.

Sharon saw them in the doorway as their gaze landed on her. She didn't need to be connected to anyone to know that they were both furious. She yanked her hand from Jadik's grip and gave him a blistering look. "How did you call them?"

He shrugged innocently and gave her a mock wounded look. He said, "Tair is my best friend," as if that explained everything.

Her glare grew hotter. She felt furious and ridiculously betrayed. "It figures! Idiots tend to stick together!"

He threw back his head and laughed. Liken and Tair reached the table and stood on each side of her. Reaching down, Liken pulled her from the chair and pinned her against his side.

She got out, "Get lost!" before Liken silenced her with a deadly, "Not one word."

She wasn't about to get into a big scene here at the restaurant with him. She, at least, could show some dignity. She would have plenty to say when they got home. She gave a curt nod. She couldn't resist saying one more word. "Fine."

Liken turned from her and said, "My thanks, Jadik. You have displayed true friendship this night."

Jadik nodded. "No thanks necessary. She is a treasure worth guarding." He turned to Tair. "I will see you soon, friend." Tair nodded and added his thanks.

Walking over to Sharon, Jadik placed a hand under her chin and raised her fuming gaze to his. "Welcome to Shimeria, Sharon Glaston. May you find pleasure," his eyes glinted, "and great happiness here." Pressing a light kiss to her mouth, he turned and joined some other men at another table.

She stood there in shock. He had kissed her casually as if he had every right. This planet was crazy. Liken began walking toward the door, pulling her along by the arm. Tair followed in their wake.

When they got outside, Sharon opened her mouth to speak. Liken stopped walking and leaned down to press a hard, tongue-thrusting kiss to her mouth. The kiss went on for a full five minutes. She tried to pull away, but that only made him jerk her hard into his body. The punishing invasion finally stopped. His voice brooked no argument. "What must be said, will be said in our home."

They stared at one another. Tair stood off to one side, patiently waiting. Sharon gave a nod of assent. The three of them started walking toward home-in silence.

Chapter Twelve

When they arrived at Liken's house, by unspoken agreement they moved into the living room. Immediately, Sharon pulled away from Liken's grasp and moved to the far side of the room, putting as much distance as possible between them. Tair turned to Liken and said, "I am glad she is safe, brother. I will leave you now."

Liken put a hand on Tair's arm. "Wait, Tair. I need you to stay."

Sharon's eyes grew wide. "Why does he need to stay for our fight?"

The two men stared at each other for a moment. Tair nodded his agreement and moved to sit on the couch. Sharon looked from one to the other as some understanding passed between the two men.

Liken said with utter calm. "You risked your safety tonight, *sherree*. There will be no fight."

She had a bad feeling about all this. She tried a placating tone. "I wasn't in any danger. Nothing happened."

Liken started walking toward her. "No, we were fortunate indeed."

He was trying to intimidate her and she wasn't going to let him get away with it. "I'm not afraid of you."

He sighed. They were less than a foot apart. "I know what you are afraid of, *sherree*. It is time you faced some of your fears." He pulled her to him and wrapped his arms around her.

She stared up into his face. It was determined with no hint of tenderness. He bent and placed his mouth over hers before she could respond.

His lips were firm and demanding. She kept her lips pressed tightly together and tried to keep her mind clear. Moving one hand to her jaw, he exerted gentle pressure. "Open your mouth, *sherree*. Now." His voice was deepening with desire.

Her mouth parted under the pressure of his hand on her jaw. He swept his tongue inside her moist warmth, thrusting deeply. She groaned and tried to put some distance between them with her hands against his chest. He removed his hand from her jaw and wrapped both arms around her, pulling her against his hard body. The kiss was overwhelming and intense. He wasn't asking for a response. He was demanding one with every thrust.

She could feel the heat spreading through her body. Her hands dropped from his chest and fisted at her sides. Her nipples tightened into hard peaks. He pressed her breasts harder into his chest in response. With a small moan, she began kissing him back. The angry words and deep hurt from their fight faded into the background of her mind as her senses took command. No matter what had been said, she hadn't stopped wanting him. He was like a fever in her blood.

Suddenly Liken tore his mouth from hers and abruptly turned her so that she was facing Tair. He was still sitting on the couch, watching the two of them with heated eyes. Under his stare, her thin blouse and skirt felt like little protection. She took a step backwards, which only brought her against Liken's hard body. He wrapped an arm around her waist instantly to hold her in place. She could feel the hard bulge of his aroused cock pressing into her lower back. She couldn't move.

Liken used his free hand to sweep her hair to one side and began nibbling on her neck. He gently bit and then licked along the sensitive nerves of her throat. Pausing near her ear, he said, "Does it matter so much, *sherree*, that he is watching us?" Her mouth went dry.

He continued his gentle assault on her throat. He tightened the arm holding her waist as his other hand lightly rubbed her stomach. She could feel the heat of his hand through the thin silk of her blouse like a burning brand. Her stomach muscles tightened in response. Her breathing sped up as she tried to squeeze more air into her lungs.

Liken's hand began climbing until it reached the underside of her left breast and paused. Sharon's body went stiff with tension. He nipped her neck a little harder. It didn't hurt, but it surprised her.

He covered her breast with his hand and gave it a gentle squeeze. His thumb began slowly circling the tight point of her nipple. The pleasure ran from her nipple in a line to her sex. She was swollen and wet. She couldn't stop the shudder that went through her. She closed her eyes.

Tair said huskily, "Open your eyes, Sharon." She was startled enough by his voice to do what he said. She saw him stand up and move toward them, his bulging arousal obvious against the front of his pants.

She felt a wave of fear, closely followed by a wave of arousal so strong her knees went weak. She leaned more heavily against Liken. Tair stopped in front of her and raised a gentle hand to caress her cheek. "Trust us, Sharon. It will go no further than you wish. The linking must be done."

Sharon could almost physically feel the arousal push away her fear. With a shaky voice, she said, "Okay." She could feel the relief in both men.

Liken gently turned her toward him. His eyes were tender, his happiness washing over her in waves. With a smile he said, "I think we'd be more comfortable on the couch."

She nodded her agreement. Liken walked to the couch and sat down. Tair followed him and sat in the chair across from the couch. She walked over to join them, wondering what would happen next.

Liken unbuttoned his shirt. As always, the sight stole the air from her. He was so beautiful. Her hands itched to feel those rippling muscles in his chest. He was reading her thoughts now because his lids lowered and he said, "You know I love to feel your hands on my chest, *sherree*."

She smiled and sat down beside him. Running her hands over him, she could feel the tension in his muscles under her fingers. She toyed with his nipples and without thinking leaned over to lick circles around one. His hand came up behind her head, tangling in her hair. He leaned into her mouth and hands with a groan. She pressed open-mouthed kisses over his chest, using her tongue to tease and taste the salty tang of his skin. He couldn't stand it for long.

With amazing speed he lifted her and brought her over his lap until she was straddling his thighs. She could feel the hard press of his cock as it strained against her through their clothes. She put her hands on his shoulders for balance and their mouths met in a long drugging kiss.

Tair's eyes burned into her back. It felt wicked and sexy. Her passion raised another notch.

Liken moved his hands up under her skirt, finding the strings of her panties. His mouth devoured hers in a searing kiss. She felt an almost imperceptible tug and then the front and back of the panties fell away. Taking the silk in his right hand, he gently pulled them out from under her.

She was completely covered by her loose skirt, but she felt exposed. Pushing down, she rubbed against his hardness. She knew he could feel her wetness through his pants, but she didn't care. It felt so good.

He arched upward to push harder against her. It brought a moan from both of them. He grabbed her hips and pulled her down onto him as he pushed up. They rocked together for a moment, simply enjoying the sensation. Liken moved his rough hands upward, warming her back with long strokes.

His hands pulled her blouse from underneath her skirt. She shuddered when she felt his hands touch the smooth skin of her naked back. She felt the heated breath of his mouth over her right nipple as he took it into his mouth and sucked. The thin silk of her blouse wasn't much of a barrier as it grew wet. She arched into his mouth, silently begging for more.

He sucked harder as his hands on her back pulled her blouse up. As she felt it rise, she pulled away and lifted her arms over her head. Once the material cleared her head, she saw him toss it by her panties on the other side of the couch. He transferred his mouth to her left breast and began licking it in teasing circles, hungry eyes watching her face.

She knew Tair was watching them, that he could see her naked back. But the pleasure she was feeling pushed all thoughts of Tair to the back of her mind. She was completely lost in Liken.

With a tortured groan, Liken pulled away from her after a few moments. Her nipples were red and wet from his mouth. She ached to have his cock inside her without the barrier of their clothes. She lifted up and pressed her hand against his arousal. "I want you." She barely recognized the husky voice as her own.

Liken moved one hand to his side and pushed a hidden button through its hole. Pulling back the fabric in the opposite direction, he then released another button on the inside. He pulled back that flap and his cock sprang into view. Sharon was impressed. "Pretty nifty."

She smiled and wrapped her fingers around him with one hand. Stroking him slowly, she watched as his face tightened with pleasure. The velvety skin of his cock felt good in her hand. He was fully erect, hard as stone. She pumped him, watching moisture bead at the tip.

He stopped her with his hand. "I must stay in control, *sherree*," he said tightly.

Lifting her up by the hips, he sat her down slowly on his erection. When he was in her to the hilt, she gave a little whimper of approval. She was full and aching with the need to move. Her hands moved to his shoulders as she lifted up. He guided her, keeping her rhythm slow and steady. Sweat beaded on his brow from his concentration. She would lift up until his cock nearly came out of her and then sink down hard. Losing herself in the pleasure, she didn't see Liken nod past her shoulder.

Tair's hands stroked her back. She went rigid with surprise. They all stopped moving. Sharon could feel Liken's cock flex inside her. He was buried to the hilt. Her gaze sought Liken's, finding only tenderness and reassurance. She took a deep breath and let it out. She leaned forward and placed a tentative kiss to Liken's mouth.

He responded and his hands on her waist began moving her again. Tair stroked her naked back, placing wet kisses along her spine. She caught fire and her skin flushed all over. The pounding of Liken's cock stroking inside her increased as their pace quickened. She was on the edge of orgasm.

Feeling the tension in her body, both men stopped and pulled back. She gritted her teeth in frustration. "Why?" She demanded an answer from Liken.

He gave her an apologetic look and lifted her completely off him. She stood there looking down at him in surprise. "What's wrong?"

Liken said quietly, "Everything is right, *sherree*, you just need to turn around."

Tair kissing and touching her back was one thing. She wasn't sure she was ready for him to see her naked breasts. She wasn't totally against the idea, she just felt nervous. Liken smiled. "It will be okay."

She squared her shoulders. Being honest with herself, she acknowledged that she was lost in the pull of her own sexuality. If she didn't want to turn around, nothing Liken said could have convinced her.

She turned around in a rush, deciding she would do it like ripping off a Band-Aid. Her gaze fell to Tair. He was sitting on the floor in front of her, looking up. His eyes darkened as he looked at her breasts. They were swollen, her red nipples jutting out from Liken's attention.

Tair raised his gaze to hers and slowly began unbuttoning his shirt. She felt Liken's hands grab her waist and position her nearly sitting in his lap facing away from him. Pushing up her skirt, he gently lowered her aching sex down onto his cock from behind. He filled her fully, stretching her inner walls, and the intense pleasure sent her climbing back toward orgasm in a hurry.

With a moan, she threw her head back, savoring the sensation of his cock deep inside her again. He began to move her up and down in an ever-increasing rhythm. Still holding her gaze, Tair slid his shirt off his shoulders. *They were both built like gods* was all she could think.

With a half smile, Tair moved forward and put a gentle hand low on her stomach over her skirt. Her stomach muscles contracted and she moaned in response. Encouraged, he drew up onto his knees and placed his hands above Liken's on her waist. The pressure was building inside her. Liken's hands fell away and then came under her arms to close over her breasts. He began to toy with her nipples.

Her hands came up and clung to Tair's shoulders in surprise as Tair's hands on her waist moved her up and down. He leaned forward and licked a path from her shoulder up the side of her neck. She felt Liken lean forward until he was nearly touching his chest to her back. Suddenly, he merged with her. She could feel the weight of his pleasure building on top of her own.

Tair's nibbling kisses moved south from her throat to the tip of one breast. Liken's hand pushed her breast upward toward Tair's tongue. Tair licked the nipple in one slow circle and then sucked it into his mouth. Looking down at him sucking on her nipple, she gave a loud moan. She couldn't take much more. They were making her crazy with need.

Liken drove his hips upward hard, just as Tair pushed her downward with equal strength. Then they both paused. With a cry, Sharon felt her body begin to pulse. Pleasure radiated in waves from her sex. She was burning from the inside out, blind and deaf to anything but the sensation of fulfillment and relief. The tension left her body in a great pouring rush.

She never even felt Tair's hands leave her waist as he wrapped his arms around her. He released her breast and moved upward. Pressing his naked chest against hers, he held her as closely as he could. Liken's hands slid to her back, making soothing motions. Gritting his teeth in frustration, Liken's face was a strained mask as he concentrated hard.

Tair put his forehead against hers and probed carefully. He had to be accurate, forceful, and quick. Sharon felt a sharp pain in her head, but it was over before she could really react. In less than a minute, both men's shoulders relaxed.

In his relief, Liken's concentration wavered and his control slipped away. He let out one long moan as his cock spurted and pulsed, sending liquid warmth inside Sharon's gripping sex. Sharon was still merged with Liken so his release sent her over the edge again.

Tair's arms tightened around her in shock. His own orgasm caught him by surprise-he hadn't come in that manner since he was a boy. They all remained motionless except for the shudders racking their bodies. The room was utterly silent except for the sounds of their ragged breathing.

Tair was the first to move. Rocking back, he sat down on the floor. With easy movements he gathered his shirt and put it back on. Sharon opened her eyes as Liken's arms came around her and squeezed gently. She felt amazingly relaxed. She ought to feel weird or guilty somehow, but she couldn't work up any concern. She felt good. There was no doubt about it.

Smiling, she levered herself off of Liken and moved to sit next to him on the couch. She grabbed her blouse and pulled it over her head. She was still wearing her skirt. She didn't bother with the panties. Liken refastened his pants. She felt his arm come around her and she put her head against his shoulder. As they all recovered, her mind began to process what had just occurred.

She had just had a sexual encounter of sorts with two men at the same time. It wasn't really a threesome in the literal sense, but she wasn't totally sure of the definition of threesome either. Deciding to think about it some other time, her thoughts drifted. Liken had given her incredible pleasure and Tair had been sexy and strangely sweet. She was so glad that it had been Tair who had linked with her and not someone else. Even Jadik.

Liken and Tair exclaimed in unison, "Jadik?!"

She glanced from one to the other in surprise. "What?"

As the name registered, she said firmly. "Both of you get out of my head right now."

Tair looked apologetic, but his voice was wry. "I will leave you as soon as my control is better, Sharon. My apologies."

He stood up. Before his shirt fell over it, Sharon noticed for the first time the large wet spot on the crotch area of his pants. Her face bloomed with color. Giving her a satisfied, lazy smile, Tair sat down in the chair across from them.

Liken's voice rumbled in her ear. "Your reference to Jadik and linking took us by surprise, *sherree*." There was a pause and then he smiled. "You had an interesting conversation with him at the eatery, did you not?"

Sharon rolled her eyes. "It takes a special kind of arrogance to just pluck something out of a person's head if you want to know what she's thinking."

Liken grinned. "I did not hear you complaining very hard earlier when we strove to please you. Did you hear any complaints, Tair?" he laughingly asked.

Tair laughed. "I think I will be going now. Sharon, your thoughts are growing louder."

Sharon laughed. They were arrogant, but she wasn't really getting angry. She felt too satisfied. The three of them stood up and walked toward the front door.

Pausing in front of the doorway, Liken reached out and gave Tair a quick hug. When Tair looked surprised, Liken said seriously, "My thanks to you, brother. We are fortunate to have your help."

Tair shrugged. "You would do the same." He turned to Sharon.

She wasn't sure if she should hug him or not. It was awkward. He solved her problem by pulling her into his arms and leaning his face close to hers. One hand cradled the back of her head and he brought his lips down to her mouth.

When she realized he meant to kiss her, she expected a brief, casual goodbye kiss. The heat of the kiss shocked her as his mobile mouth took her by storm. She responded without thought even when his tongue thrust against hers. He pulled back and smiled. She was dazed and breathless again. She couldn't think of a single thing to say.

He gave a husky laugh. "Welcome to Shimeria, Sharon. I am honored to be your link."

She said weakly, "Thanks." This planet was one surprise after another.

Liken and Tair both laughed. Tair walked through the doorway and headed into the silvery night. Liken pressed the button and the wall slid soundlessly shut.

Putting his arm back around her shoulders, Liken began walking Sharon toward the bedroom. His voice was still amused as he said, "Relax, *sherree*. The linking relationship is not complicated. Tair will kiss you, but only in greeting, and it will never go further than that. It is a harmless thing, a benefit for providing protection."

A horrifying thought struck her. "Are you and Tair linked? How did you…"

He couldn't help it. She looked so repulsed. He laughed. "Yes, Sharon, but two Shimerian males do not link in the way you just did with Tair. We simply drop our shields and establish a mutual link. It requires a great deal of trust."

So, the weird linking relationship was because she was female and not a Shimerian male. She and Tair were linked and that meant they had a kind of casually intimate relationship. Liken wasn't jealous at all. She wasn't sure how she felt about that.

Liken and Tair made it seem so natural. Sexuality on Shimeria was very different. Even Jadik had kissed her and that was okay. But Liken had seemed jealous when other males paid her too much attention, like in the eatery. Could things get any more confusing?

When they reached their bedroom, she sank down on the bed. She wasn't going to think about the bizarre customs of Shimeria. She'd sort it all out tomorrow. She wasn't going to worry about it tonight.

Liken sat down beside her and bent down for a kiss. His mouth paused over hers as he whispered, "There will be no worrying, *sherree*. You will experience only pleasure this eve."

And true to his word, he spent the rest of the night proving it.

Chapter Thirteen

The next morning Sharon murmured sleepy objections when Liken gently shook her shoulder. She was exhausted. She heard a low chuckle next to her ear.

Liken said, "*Sherree*, I know you are too tired for loveplay. Please open your eyes for a moment."

Her lids felt like lead weights as she gradually came awake and opened her eyes. He was sitting on the edge of the bed, smiling down at her. She smiled back and said, "Good morning."

His smile broadened. "Indeed it is." He placed a soft kiss on her mouth. Drawing back, he looked regretful. "I am sorry to wake you, Sharon, but I must leave for a time. A few matters at my workplace require immediate attention. It was unexpected. I am sorry but it is something I must handle."

"An emergency?" she asked, still half asleep.

"No emergency. Just a few details that cannot wait until after our knowing period." His voice was filled with regret.

She nodded her understanding. Her sleepy brain was beginning to function. "It's no problem. I'll just drop by the library or something." A thought struck her. "Liken, can I ask you to do something for me today?"

He nodded before she even finished her question. "What is it, *sherree*?"

Memories of yesterday were beginning to swirl in her head. The lovemaking and the fighting. She needed some time alone to process them. She needed some space. She needed him out of her head, but she didn't want to disturb their fragile peace. She raised unconsciously pleading eyes to his face.

His eyes turned tender and he gave a half laugh. "When you look at me with those eyes, *sherree*, you can have whatever you want."

Sharon said carefully, "I don't want to hurt your feelings, but I've got a lot to think about today. A lot has happened in the last ten days. I really need some time to myself, okay? I mean, I don't want to be self-conscious, worrying about you randomly tuning into my thoughts."

He sighed. "I understand, but I do not scan your thoughts for entertainment, Sharon. It is the way of my people. It is a special closeness that lovers share. I wish you would become more comfortable with it."

She said softly, "Maybe I will if I have some time to sort it through. I don't know."

He nodded. "I will withdraw and block you if that is your wish. At least for today. You have my oath."

Sharon knew that if he gave his word, he would abide by it. His emotions told her that he wanted to keep contact, but would do as she asked-for today, anyway. She gave him a smile of gratitude and said softly, "Thanks... It means a lot to me."

He leaned down and kissed her slowly. It was a sweetly searching kiss, strangely different from any other they had shared. They lingered, mouths seeming to convey things they couldn't put into words. When they slowly pulled apart, they stared at each other silently for a moment.

Finally, Liken cleared his throat. "I will return before evemeal, *sherree*, perhaps sooner. Enjoy this day." His hand caressed her face and then he turned and left the room. She could hear the front door sliding closed a moment later.

She sat up and moved to the edge of the bed. Standing, she walked to the far side of the room. Pressing a button on the wall, she stared at a hologram of herself. Like the one at the shop, it served as a mirror. It was nice to have one at home, although she was still growing used to it. More than once, she had been startled by the three-dimensional depiction of herself. It was like having an identical twin mirroring her every move.

Today, the image greeting her didn't look like her twin. She was staring at a stranger. The woman facing her looked nothing like the Sharon Glaston she knew. Her dark hair was tumbled around a face with glowing eyes and swollen lips. Her nude body had small red marks from a night of passion. She looked rumpled and strangely sexy. The passionate creature staring back at her looked powerfully female and mysterious.

Sharon backed away and sat down hard on the bed. Her image stayed in her mind. She was that woman. Maybe she had always been that woman and it had taken Liken to make her see it. He had ripped her out of her safe little world and stripped away that protective outer shell that she presented to everyone around her.

She had always thought of herself as a cautious woman who was content to lead a rather routine life. She was everyone's dependable friend, the person who could be counted on to be reasonable. Other people led lives of messy emotion. She was the one that could be relied upon to help them clean up the mess.

She was stable and structured and even a little boring in some ways. No surprises, no real passion, and no real pain. But underneath all that lived a woman who could rage and fight and hurt like anyone else. A woman who could be passionate and difficult and not at all reasonable. A woman who could love deeply.

Sharon's head dropped to her hands. There, that was the crux of it. People who loved deeply risked being hurt deeply. And in the last ten days, she had fallen passionately, deeply, foolishly in love with Liken. There was nothing cautious or reasonable about it. It was utterly ridiculous. It made absolutely no sense, but it was undeniable.

He made her feel out of control. He challenged her and seduced her and pushed her at every turn. It was frightening, but she had never felt so alive in her life. He was arrogant and domineering at times. He could be sweetly tender and giving. Physically, he was a fantasy male come to life.

Sometimes, he understood her better than she understood herself. At other times, she wondered if he knew her at all. All she knew was that the last ten days had been the most incredible, happiest, most confusing days of her life. And she didn't want it to end. She wanted to spend the rest of her life loving and fighting with Liken.

She thought of the library on Earth, her job, her friends. She knew she could get a job on Shimeria, probably even at the local Earth library with Gar. Her heart twisted in her chest at the thought of being separated from Kate. More than anything right now she wished Kate were here so that she could talk to her and tell her how she felt. Of course, if Tair had his way, Kate might be living here, too. She cheered at that thought.

The bottom line, though, wasn't whether she should give up her old life or not. The bottom line was whether she had the guts to step out on a very high limb. She would have to start a new life on an alien planet with a man she loved-a man who might or might not love her back.

She thought sometimes he did love her. When he looked at her with such melting tenderness, she could almost believe it. But, at other times, she felt like a possession he had claimed and wouldn't give up. He had tried very hard to make her happy, but she wasn't sure if it was to make her stay or if he loved her enough to want to see her happy.

She had felt his affection and happiness run through her many times. She could make him happy in the long run. She was almost sure of it. They could have a good life together. Did she have the guts to try?

Sharon felt her heart pound at the thought. She had come to a strange planet. She had slept with an alien and eaten weird food. She had yelled and cussed and been completely unreasonable at times. She had two men with a doorway into her head, and a near threesome under her belt. Did she have the guts to grab her own happiness? Hell, yes she did!

Her head came up and a huge smile filled her face. The old Sharon would have stayed sitting on the bed half the day, listing all of the reasons why it was a bad idea to let emotion rule. The new Sharon stood up and headed for the bathroom. She was going to see Liken and tell him she was staying. She was going to risk everything and tell him she loved him.

Her confident steps faltered as she thought of his reaction. What if he stared at her blankly, or worse, uneasily thanked her in response? Well, then, she'd just have to kill him.

She strode into the bathroom like a soldier headed off to battle. Kate would have applauded.

Chapter Fourteen

An hour later, having eaten and showered, she headed out the front door dressed in a shimmering blue blouse and skirt. It was the outfit they had purchased during their shopping trip. She didn't care if the outfit was more revealing than anything she had ever worn on Earth. Besides, she knew it was the most flattering thing she owned. Her hair was gleaming around her shoulders and she felt ready to take on the world.

She had seen Liken's office a few days ago. On one of their trips into town, he had taken her by and given her a tour of the place. His coworkers had been curious about her, but unfailingly gracious and charming. Their respect and affection for Liken had been apparent.

Sharon had considered waiting until he returned home from the office in the afternoon, but had decided against it. She had made her decision and was eager to forge ahead. Besides, being impulsive for a change wasn't a bad thing. Liken's work hadn't sounded critical, merely something minor that couldn't be put off. She would surprise him with her visit and give him a good reason to rush home.

Entering the building where he worked, she began walking toward his office in the back. A few people smiled and greeted her, but she answered them with brief, friendly responses and kept walking. She couldn't wait to see Liken. She reached the doorway of his office and felt her entire body turn rigid with disbelief.

Liken was embracing a petite redhead. His mouth was moving over hers with gentle hunger and she was responding with enthusiasm. She could feel his tenderness for the woman run through her in one long wave. Sharon's mind blanked. A pain so sharp it felt fatal hit her in the chest. Disillusionment and agony cut her to the bone. When she could draw a breath, the words tumbled out from her mind to her mouth without a second in between.

"You cheating bastard." Her voice was actually soft, but his head came up with a snap. She must have screamed it in her mind because he winced in pain and brought a hand to his head. He looked shocked to see her. The redhead turned in surprise. Sharon's face was without an ounce of color. Her voice shook as she said, "I thought I would surprise you by showing up. I guess I did."

Liken took a step toward her, but she threw up her hand in response. He spoke her name, "Sharon…" but that was all he had time to get out before she spoke again.

"So you had to go into the office today, huh?" She looked at the redhead, who was beginning to frown in confusion. She said flatly, "I'm his pactmate." The woman's eyes widened.

Sharon felt a welcoming numbness spread through her, overcoming the pain. Liken said firmly, "Sharon, you must listen to me…"

She cut him off. "No, I don't need to listen." Looking at the redhead, she said, "You're welcome to the faithless asshole. Enjoy him while you can." She looked back at Liken. "You can go to hell." With fragile dignity, she turned and started walking away quickly.

She heard the woman say "Liken?" in a throaty, questioning voice. His voice murmured in response.

She sped up. Reaching the doorway of the building, she started to run. She could hear his voice behind her yelling, "Sharon, wait!" but she didn't stop. She kept running, taking side paths at random, one after another, wanting only to escape.

She ran until her legs ached and her vision was too blurred to see where she was going. She finally stopped and looked around. She was in the park area. Walking to a tree with huge red leaves, she sat down under it and drew her knees to her chest. She took gasping breaths and stared blindly ahead. She couldn't even cry. The shock and pain were so deep that her chest hurt, but her eyes remained dry. She sat in rigid silence, totally unaware of her surroundings.

Her mind raced in frantic circles as she strove to block the image of Liken and the redhead from her mind. He had feelings for that woman. That kiss was not platonic. It had been passionate. And she had been on her way to tell him...

The first edge of anger shot through her. And he had been... He was a bastard, plain and simple.

Her nostrils flared. Fuck risking and destiny, and most especially fuck that cheating Liken.

Chapter Fifteen

Liken was sitting in his office alone when Tair appeared in the doorway. Leaning back in the chair, he said wearily in English, "Hello, brother."

Tair leaned negligently against the frame. "Hello, brother?" he echoed. "Is that all you wish to say?"

Liken arched an eyebrow. "What is it you expect me to say?"

Tair shook his head and walked across the office, dropping into the chair across from Liken. "I do not know. It seems so mundane when your pactmate has been screaming in my head."

Looking at Liken closely, his eyes widened. "You, however, are conveniently blocking her and are left unaffected."

Liken laughed, although it sounded hollow. "Unaffected? You are wrong. Nonetheless, I am blocking her because I gave oath that I would not scan her thoughts this day."

His brother was an idiot. Tair gave him an amazed look. "Why would you do such a thing?"

"She wanted privacy to sort out her thinking, she said." Liken sounded as if the weight of the world pressed him from all sides.

Tair gave a snort. What a mess. "Well, I believe she needs to do a great deal more sorting now. She believes you have betrayed her with Elana."

Liken felt the pain of it strike home. "I know." He kept seeing her face in his mind. When he had looked at her, the agony and distrust on her face had struck him like a blow. He had stood there in shock unable to move or to think. In that moment he had believed she was lost to him forever. She would never trust him enough to stay.

He could bind her to him sexually. He could physically keep her with him. But he could not force her to love him or trust him. She had to give it freely. He felt helpless and confused.

When they had taken the oath, he arrogantly thought he could make her want to stay. He was a Shimerian warrior, a guardian, used to righting wrongs and winning. She was a woman, physically smaller and weaker. She was inexperienced sexually and would be easily seduced. She would give up her old life and make a life with him on Shimeria. He would make her want him and want this life.

Now those thoughts seemed foolish and amazingly selfish. He couldn't force her to love him or trust him. She would not stay without those things. The realization was devastating and humbling.

Tair sighed. This pactmate business was trickier than it had seemed. He asked, "What are you going to do?"

Liken shrugged. "I will give her time and then we shall see." He couldn't seem to get the look on her face out of his mind.

It was Tair's turn to lift an eyebrow. "She is hurting, thinking the worst. Do you not care?"

Liken's glare would have knocked a lesser man than Tair from his seat. "She brings pain to herself with her own distrust. I will explain later."

Tair knew his brother enough to comprehend the real hurt underneath that anger. He said quietly, "I think your own wounds prevent you from seeking to heal hers."

The accusation was pure truth and Liken couldn't deny it. "True enough. I am angry. She should have asked for an explanation instead of assuming the worst."

Tair laughed. His voice rang with skepticism, "As you would have done if you had found her kissing an unknown male?"

Liken felt instant rage at the mere thought. "I would not have left without demanding answers."

Tair made a mock sound of sudden discovery and said, "Ahhhh. So you were doubly wounded. That dignified exit was lowering, was it?"

Liken looked and sounded defeated as he said, "She was so controlled. No woman who loves a man could have acted in that manner."

Tair's face was sympathetic, but his eyes were amused. "Why would you care? She does not have to love you to stay and be pledged. She is but a woman."

Liken's voice was just short of a yell. "I love her! Are you satisfied? Will you cease this endless prodding?"

She was beautiful and frustrating and intelligent and stupid. She made him angry, she made him laugh, and she made him ache with sweet pleasure. She was perfect and riddled with faults and everything in between. He would love her until his dying breath, and probably beyond it. It infuriated him. She infuriated him.

Tair laughed, not unkindly. "At last. I was about to lose all hope for you, brother. Now, let us see if we can get past those wounds to the truth. Why would she hurt so much if she had no love for you?"

The words pierced Liken's emotions and cleared his mind. "Why, indeed?" His heart lifted. She had to love him to react so strongly.

He felt another wave of pain at the thought of her distrust. "She may love me, but she does not trust me. I think she does not even trust herself."

Tair sighed. "True enough. I am out of questions and answers, brother. Would you like me to find her and bring her to you?" As their link, he was responsible for her protection, but volunteering was really more of an impulse to help.

Liken shook his head. "No. It seems now I am the one who must sort through his thoughts. She will come home when she is ready. She is much stronger and more passionate than she thinks. She will demand answers. I have no doubt. Would you just watch over her until then? Make sure she is all right?"

"Of course," Tair replied. He hated to think that Liken and Sharon might not work their problems out. They were perfect for each other, even if they didn't seem to understand it yet. He asked, "And will your answers persuade her to stay? Will she trust you?"

Liken stared at his brother. "I guess that is one question only time will answer." At the moment, the thought was not encouraging.

Chapter Sixteen

Sharon sat under the tree for quite some time. Several hours passed as thoughts swirled like a storm in her head. Eventually, the pain settled like an aching weight in her chest but her mind had cleared somewhat.

She couldn't reconcile Liken lying to her and making love with another woman while committed to her. He had been honest with her in the past, although not always forthright. She would have bet her life that he was a faithful, honorable man. In a way, she had bet her life. Her new life.

It didn't make sense. Fury filled her. Since she'd stepped onto this planet, a lot of things hadn't made sense. It had been one surprise after another. She had found herself and risked everything and been crushed in the end. Well, she could crawl back into her shell and never come out. Or she could get back up, and face him and demand a few answers. If she turned messy, and emotional, and ugly, then he would just have to deal with it. He had broken her heart, but she would survive it.

She wasn't going back to the person she had been before him. She wasn't running from anyone or anything ever again. Being cautious and reasonable might produce a safe and comfortable life, but she wanted more than safety. She deserved more. And she would have it. Even without Liken.

Her eyes focused on her surroundings for the first time. She recognized where she was and felt a quick pang of relief that she was in the park and could find her way home. She stood up. Tair stepped out from the shadows of a huge tree to her right. She was startled. "How long have you been there?"

He shrugged in response. His face was a remote mask. "I will escort you home."

"I don't need an escort." Her voice was sharper than she meant it to be. "I know the way."

He stared at her with a coolness that was chilling. "Nonetheless, I will walk with you."

She had no idea what he was thinking or feeling. He seemed distant and unapproachable. Now it was her turn to shrug. "Fine."

They turned and began walking. When he remained silent beside her, she angled her head up at him and frowned. She was the injured party here. "What's your problem?"

Again, he leveled her with that chilling gaze. He remained silent. She said coolly, "Whatever." She would deal with Tair after she dealt with Liken. She was saving all her energy for the confrontation with Liken.

They walked in silence until they reached the pathway to the house. As they approached the doorway, Tair paused and put a hand on her arm. She stopped and turned to face him with a questioning glance. He searched her face and then said with cool precision, "You never greeted me. You will do so now."

"What?" She was totally confused.

He smiled grimly. "I am your link. You never greeted me, Sharon."

Her eyes widened in response and her mouth fell open a little in surprise. He wanted her to kiss him? Now?

His mouth came down on hers ruthlessly before she had a chance to respond. He thrust his tongue past her parted lips and explored her mouth like he owned it. Her hands came up to his chest to reflexively push him away. He merely wrapped his arms around her tightly and continued the punishing kiss.

She realized that her heart hadn't been carved out of her chest. It was beating frantically. She could feel treacherous arousal begin to spread through her body. Without conscious thought, her lips and tongue began a dance of response. She wanted him, but only in a physical sense. She didn't love him.

He wasn't Liken. Just the thought of Liken and the pain in her chest ached like a dull tooth. The kiss gentled, and finally, he lifted his head. "You will remember this."

She was totally confused again. "What?" Did he mean remember him after she left for Earth?

His smile was wicked and the warmth had come back into his eyes. This was the Tair she remembered well, not the cold, cruel man from the eatery. "Goodbye, Sharon." He walked away from her in the direction of town.

Sharon stood there, feeling perplexed. Mentally throwing up her hands, she turned and walked to the front door. She hit the button and it slipped open in immediate response. She braced herself and walked in.

Walking into the living room, she saw Liken casually sitting on the sofa. He looked up at her and raised an eyebrow as she strode to the center of the room. He didn't look upset. He looked perfectly calm.

How could he look so normal when she was dying inside? It was the last insult to her battered heart. Her voice could have cut glass. "I am going to discuss this morning with you. While we do it, you are keeping your hands to yourself. When we're done here, you're packing a few things and staying somewhere else. With Tair or with your girlfriend, I really don't care. But you are not touching me again. On the twenty-first, we'll go back and file incompatible. I deserve better than a faithless liar."

His face never changed. They might have been discussing the weather. It pushed her fury up a notch.

With infuriating calm, he said, "You want to discuss this morning. What is there to say?"

His voice was soft, so even-tempered, and she could not feel a trace of emotion coming from him. She could feel the dam holding her temper spring several leaks. "I'm your pactmate. How could you be with someone else? You may not love me, but you should have had enough respect for me to..."

He cut her off. "You want to talk of love and respect?" He gave a cynical laugh. "Perhaps we should begin by speaking of trust."

Her voice rose. "Maybe we should. I trusted you, you bastard!"

Suddenly, she realized Liken was not as calm as she had assumed. He was sitting on the sofa, but the hand resting on the arm was gripping it so hard his knuckles were white. It was the only warning she had of his real state before he burst into motion.

He sprang from the couch and grabbed her by the arms. She looked up into his face and saw pure fury. He shouted, "You know nothing of trust!"

She felt the dam burst open and white-hot fury broke free. "I know you were kissing that redhead and enjoying it! I know you have feelings for her! I know I feel like a fool and it's your fault! I know you're an asshole! Take your hands off of me!"

His face went white. "I will touch you whenever I like. I will do whatever I like! I am your pactmate!"

"And she's your lover!" The accusation rang in the silence of the room.

He shook her until her teeth rattled, then abruptly let her go. Taking a step back, he said flatly, "I am her link."

The words took a moment to register. As he stared at her in furious silence, she echoed, "Her link?"

He gave one swift nod. "Yes, her link. Her name is Elana and she has been pledged to my friend, Revka, for over three years now."

"But you love her...and you were kissing her..." Her anger was fading into confusion.

He told her grimly, "I do not love her, at least not in the sense you mean. I am her link. I care for her as Tair cares for you."

Suddenly, the little scene with Tair outside the house took on a new meaning. His words ran through her mind again. "I am your link. You did not greet me. Remember this…"

"Are you saying she was greeting you, that you've never had sex with her?" She couldn't keep the doubt from her voice.

He looked exasperated. "Yes, she was greeting me. As for sex with her, it was on one occasion during the initial link."

When Sharon would have responded, he lifted an eyebrow and said, "Not everyone is as uncomfortable with the thought of a threesome. The linking process is different depending on the participants."

Sharon felt the color rise in her face. Her heart picked up speed as she suddenly focused on something he said earlier. "You don't love her."

She nearly sagged with relief. He wasn't in love with the redhead. The truth in his voice had been obvious. She believed him.

She thought of Liken's lack of jealousy regarding her actions with Tair. Shimerian culture was very different from Earth. The linking partners shared intimacy but it was not considered a threat or a betrayal. She felt the last of her anger die. Embarrassment and sorrow rose up in its place.

"I'm sorry. I didn't know." She felt guilty as she considered what had happened from Liken's point of view. She hadn't trusted him, hadn't even let him explain. Her hurt and anger had been too great.

He nodded stiffly. "You could not know. You did not wait for an explanation."

The accusation in his voice was easy to hear, but she could feel anger radiating from him without it. Underneath the anger was a layer of hurt. She had hurt him. She was surprised at how much her distrust had hurt him.

She stepped forward and placed a tentative hand on his chest. "Liken, I really am sorry. I couldn't think. I was just so hurt and angry." She thought she detected a slight relaxation of his tense shoulders at the sincerity in her voice.

He sighed, and his face lost some of its grimness. "You have no cause for jealousy, Sharon." He sounded tired now. "Why were you at the office today?"

Sharon swallowed. Here was the tough part. Her emotions felt raw. She had been on a roller coaster of feeling today, and she was worn out by the experience. "I wanted to talk to you." She wasn't going to chicken out, but she needed a moment to work up her nerve. His hurt was proof he loved her, at least a little. She had to take the risk and be honest.

He continued to stare at her in silence. Sharon tilted her head back further to get a better look at his eyes. He looked impatient. Taking a deep breath, she let it out in a rush. "I came to the office because I wanted to tell you that I love you. I want to stay. I'll pledge with you."

He looked like she had hit him on the head with a shovel. When he continued to stare at her, dumbfounded, she felt her nerves leap. "I mean, if you want me to stay. I…"

He wrapped his arms around her and squeezed the rest of her words right out of her. His voice boomed next to her ear. "How could you think I would not want you to stay?"

The pressure in her chest lightened. He really wanted her to stay. He hadn't said he loved her, but it was a beginning. She leaned back and peered up at him. "I'm sorry, but I've been so confused. When I saw you kissing her, I just…"

He gave her a hard look. "Yes, I know what you thought." Some of the warmth left his face. "Yet, as always, you were so very controlled. You did not stay and demand answers. You did not make a scene. You might have lost your precious control."

The accusation hurt. "You have no idea how I felt…"

"No, I do not. How could I? You left." His hands came up to her shoulders. She could feel a new tension in him. "Tell me, *sherree*, what would happen if you gave up that control of yours. Why does it frighten you so much? Would it be so terrible?"

Unease spread through her body. Where was he going with his comments? "I don't know."

He shook his head. "I think you do. I think you cannot trust enough to give that much of yourself. You say you love me, but do you trust me enough to truly lose all control with me? To show me yourself?"

He was scaring her, but she was honest enough to admit he could be right. The safe thing to do would be to take a step back from him and end this discussion now. She wasn't going to do it. She was through playing it safe. "I don't know, but I'll try."

His smile held a cruel edge. She knew he wasn't going to make it easy for her, not when she had hurt him so badly this morning. "Then we shall see."

Liken turned from her, not wanting her to see the hope on his face. Would she really give him her trust? Thoughts of her dark fantasies flashed through his mind. Walking across the room, he sat down on the couch. "Remove your clothing. Now." His voice was firm, as if he expected some resistance.

She felt a shimmer of nerves. To her embarrassment, she could feel a growing arousal at his tone. He was going to try to take control and dominate her sexually, she knew. It went against her every feminist principle, but the thought didn't stop the warmth spreading through her. She wanted him. Even more, she wanted him like this.

Taking a deep breath, she brought her hands to her blouse and drew it over her head. She tossed it to the floor. She could feel his heated gaze watching her every movement. Her nipples tightened under his gaze. She bent down and hurriedly began to take off the skirt.

His voice was cool and distant, a direct contrast to the heat in his eyes. "Turn around. Take it off slowly."

She turned around and began sliding the skirt over her hips. She was left only in her skimpy panties, facing away from him. She turned around to see his face.

"I did not tell you to turn around, *sherree*, did I?" He sounded angry.

She shook her head. "I just wanted…"

His smile made her nerves jump again. "I know what you want. I have been inside that mind of yours, remember? You have quite an interesting fantasy life. I believe it is time for us to explore some of those dark little secrets." He motioned her forward. "Come to me."

As she walked across the room, she was acutely aware of her exposed body. At the mention of her fantasies, a dark thrill had gone through her. She could feel herself blushing. Stopping in front of him, she waited for his next move.

"So willing, *sherree*. I am impressed." His voice was faintly mocking. He grew serious again. "Lay facedown across my lap."

No, she wasn't going to do it. She could feel the moistness between her thighs and was mortified. She was not going to lie across his lap. Would he really spank her because she had turned around? Or because of her distrust this morning? Shame warred with arousal. She shook her head.

His eyes were as hard as his voice. "Do it."

Cheeks burning, she shook her head. "No."

Reaching out roughly, he pulled her downward until she collapsed on his lap. Squirming, she tried to break free, but he was too strong. Eventually, she found herself draped across his lap, staring down at the floor. She protested. "This is ridiculous. Let me up. What do you think you're doing? Are you crazy?"

The hard pressure of his hand on her back kept her down. His other hand came down with a light tap on her ass. "Be still."

She was shocked. He'd actually done it. She went still from surprise.

She heard his low chuckle. "Very good, *sherree*." He raised his hand and delivered another couple of smacks. He wasn't hurting her, but she felt her bottom begin to grow warm. With a sense of embarrassment, she felt the wetness between her legs grow, too. She squirmed.

The hand on her back grew heavier as he kept her in place. "You still think you have some choice, I see. Perhaps I should make myself clearer." She felt a tug on each side of her panties as he released the strings. Cool air brushed against the warm cheeks of her bottom as he lifted the back of the panties away. She was exposed.

She felt his rough hand lightly caress one pink cheek. Suddenly, he moved his hand up and he began lightly spanking her again. The minor sting of his hand was nothing compared to the heat blooming inside her. She couldn't understand it. She was trembling with excitement and nerves.

Suddenly, he stopped. His hand lightly traced her bottom. His voice sounded husky, but it was still firm. "At this moment, you are wondering what I will do to you. What you will let me do to you."

His hand moved lower and he trailed one finger along the wetness of her thighs. "You are so wet." Her body tensed as he lazily drew that finger upward toward her sex. He teased her swollen lips and then probed gently inside. With a moan, she went limp.

"That's it, *sherree*. I can feel your walls clinging to me. Tighten around my finger." He brought the rest of his fingers under her and began circling her clit. It was exquisite torture. She felt him pressing and playing with her. The finger inside her began moving in and out. She let out a whimper of need. It felt so good, but she wanted his hard cock in place of his finger.

Bringing her head up and turning, she could see his hard cock straining within his pants. "I want you inside me."

He withdrew his finger from inside her and trailed it along her swollen lips again. "Do you?" His finger left a trail of wetness in its wake as it slowly climbed upward between the cheeks of her bottom. Reaching the tight bud of her ass, he lightly touched the knot of nerves. "Where?"

Oh no. She was not into anal sex. No way. Her body tensed instinctively. She made a strangled sound of protest.

He laughed. "Nervous, *sherree*? I am in control here, remember? You have no control. I can fuck you any way I like." He continued to tickle that tight ring of nerves with light strokes of his wet finger.

Her sudden twisting motion away from him nearly sent her sprawling to the floor. She landed on her knees and began to stand up. Her panties fell away, and she was naked, standing in front of him.

Like lightning, he grabbed her hips and brought her forward to his mouth. Her knees went weak as she felt the stroking heat of his tongue across her clit. She closed her eyes and her head went back. It was too much. He sucked and circled, and probed delicately until she was moaning with the pleasure. Suddenly, the incredible sensations stopped. She opened her eyes.

Liken stood and looked at her with the eyes of a hungry predator. She took an instinctive step backward in surprise. He smiled. He took a step forward and then grabbed her. His movements were rough, but the hands on her arms were gentle as he turned her and walked her around to the back of the chair. Pushing her facedown over the back of it, he put one hand on her back to hold her down.

The rustle of his clothing as he unbuttoned his pants was the only sound in the room. With no other warning, his hard cock thrust into her aching sex. He began pumping in and out of her roughly. She felt her whole body catch fire. She began to push her hips back against him to meet his strokes. He brought one hand down into stinging contact with her bottom. His voice was firm. "No."

She stopped in surprise, but let out a moan of protest. He brought one hand forward and began to toy with her right nipple. His rhythm remained ruthlessly steady even when he said softly, "You will not come until I allow it."

The tug on her nipple was a passionate torment. She ached with it. She was growing frustrated at the slow rhythm of his thrusts. She arched her back to take him deeper. She wanted more, damn it.

He knew what she wanted, but he was the one in control. He had the nerve to laugh. "No, *sherree*."

She felt another stinging tap. Anger was beginning to mix with need. "Faster. Go faster and deeper." She wasn't sure if it was a demand or a plea.

He responded by slowing and gentling his thrusts. "Ask me nicely and I will consider it." His mocking tone deliberately provoked her.

She could feel her temper straining and struggled to rein it in. "Go to hell. I don't want this anymore. Let me up!"

He thrust his cock all the way into her, in one hard thrust. Buried to the hilt, he brought his fingers from her nipple down to her sex. He found her clit and began teasing it. "What is wrong, *sherree*? Will you beg me to continue or to stop?" His mocking tone said he knew she wouldn't ask him to stop.

She wanted to demand that he stop immediately, but he was filling her and pressing against her clit with such skill. "Bastard."

He laughed again. "Your language is deteriorating, Sharon." He gave her a couple of hard, deep thrusts in reward.

She moaned and pushed against him, fighting for each stroke of his cock. The war waged for some time. She was getting desperate for release. Frustration, passion, and anger were raging inside her. Each time she grew close, he would pull back and then change rhythms. It was maddening.

She spat angry words in between strokes. "You're driving me crazy. Cut it out! I mean it. You fucking tease."

His only response was another slap to her bottom as he continued the torment. His hand on her hip moved and he trailed one finger between the cheeks of her bottom. Drawing moisture from below, he circled her tight bud with teasing strokes.

She went hot and then cold. He wouldn't. She had no sooner thought it, then she felt a gentle probing pressure as his finger dipped inside slightly. It was foreign and scary, and she was ashamed to admit, exciting. It didn't hurt, but she felt the last shred of her control snap away. She let out a scream of sheer frustration.

As if he had been waiting for that sound, he merged with her in one hard push. The feel of his pleasure mixing with hers sent her right to the edge. She was terrified he would stop. "Don't stop."

His voice was dark with need. "Ask me to fuck you harder." It was an order.

"Please fuck me harder." Need was clawing at her. She was completely out of control.

"Swear you'll never leave." He ruthlessly pounded his cock into her sex.

"I swear it." She almost screamed the words.

"You're mine. I can do anything, have anything I want." His thrusts became faster and she was moaning over and over.

"Yes, anything…"

He spoke through gritted teeth, "Then come for me." His finger on her clit pressed inward as he arched his spine to add strength to his thrusts.

Her scream echoed loudly as she shattered into a million pieces. Her lower body clenched and pulsed around his cock and his still embedded finger. With a loud groan, he lost control and found his own release.

He fell forward and leaned against her back, his big body covering hers. His hands came around her to gently stroke her breasts.

Sharon lay beneath Liken, too exhausted to move. She felt hollow inside, as if someone had come in and swept everything away. It was strangely peaceful. She felt totally vulnerable and exposed in a way that had nothing to do with her body's nakedness. She loved Liken and needed him and had no defenses against it.

She felt tears on her face and realized with a sniff that she was crying. She had lost all control, acted like an animal, and the world hadn't ended. Liken was still holding her, pressing gentle kisses to the side of her neck. She felt his feelings run through her. His tenderness, his warmth, and his love wrapped around her. Realizing he did love her brought on a flood of fresh tears.

Liken grew aware that Sharon was crying beneath him. He quickly rose up and turned her over with concern. Tears were streaming down her face. Looking horrified, he picked her up in his arms and carried her to the couch. "Sharon, did I hurt you?"

She shook her head and tried to say no, but only sobbing sounds came out. She ducked her head into his chest and wept.

Liken wrapped gentle arms around her and tried to understand. He was relieved he hadn't hurt her, but he couldn't understand why she was crying. Sharon never cried. She had come to his planet and confronted massive changes without shedding one tear. Now, suddenly, she was sobbing as if her heart was broken. He thought about scanning her thoughts, but remembered his promise.

With dismay, he wondered if he had pushed her too far too fast. Rubbing her back as she sobbed in his arms, he ached at the sight and sound of her tears. He whispered, "*Sherree*, please…you are killing me with your tears…I am sorry… Please tell me what has hurt you. I love you. I cannot bear to see you hurting." His words of comfort continued, in both Shimerian and English, but Sharon was too shattered to respond.

Finally, she pulled away from his chest and tried to get herself under control. She felt free suddenly. She knew she was naked in the arms of a nearly fully clothed man. Her hair was a tangled mess, and her face was splotchy with tears. Her nose was running and she looked horrible.

Gone was the cautious, tidy, undemanding Sharon. The end result wasn't as pretty maybe, but it was honest. Her life was in shambles, but she had found herself and someone who loved her in the midst of total chaos. It was everything she had avoided, and at the same time, everything she had secretly wanted. "I love you, too. It's okay. You didn't hurt me. I just feel relieved and overwhelmed."

He had been in her mind for nearly two weeks and he still could not understand her. She was a mystery to him, one he hoped to spend his life solving. "I do not understand. You are crying in relief?" It made no sense.

Sharon gave him a shaky smile. "I'm fine."

He shook his head. "I think you are still hurting because of this morning. I am sorry I did not come after you and explain about Elana."

"No, really. I do understand. And I'm sorry I didn't trust you enough to ask for explanations. I had gotten my nerve up to risk telling you about my feelings and seeing you with her just shocked and destroyed me."

He pressed a gentle kiss to her mouth. "*Sherree*, there are things in our cultures that are vastly different. I know that there are adjustments we both will have to make. I have been arrogant in thinking all the adjustments would be yours. We will work together to solve any problems that arise. If the kissing makes you unhappy, I do not understand it but out of respect I will not do it." It was said as a promise.

Sharon placed a hand to his cheek. "We love each other. We trust each other. We can face whatever we have to face together."

Liken's arms tightened. "I am so fortunate to have found you, *sherree*. I want a life with you and children. I want to make you happy."

Sharon's smile was blinding. "I wouldn't mind a few little Likens myself. And you do make me happy."

Their mouths met in a kiss of wonder and love. When at last they pulled apart, Sharon dropped her hand and began unbuttoning Liken's shirt. With a playful grin, she said, "Now, let's talk about this tendency you have to dominate me in bed."

He let out a satisfied laugh. "I am a Shimerian male, am I not? Do not pretend you dislike it, *sherree*. I know otherwise. I know all kinds of interesting, dark fantasies you ache to explore. Would you like to discuss them?"

She felt heat rise to her cheeks as she finished the last of the buttons. Spreading his shirt, she leaned forward and swirled her tongue around one of his nipples. She could feel his big body tense. Her husky voice dripped satisfaction as she said, "Nope, I believe it's my turn for a little revenge."

She placed teasing kisses in a steady downward path. Peeking up at him through her lashes, she watched his eyes darken with arousal. She paused and unbuttoned his pants. He went completely still under her hands. "You'll have to adjust. ."

Liken watched the dark curtain of her hair lower over his lap. When her mouth closed over his aching cock, he couldn't stifle his moan. He could feel the blood leaving his head and heading south.

Bringing his hands to tangle in her hair, he arched upward helplessly. He had one last thought before his mind went completely blank. She was a librarian, for goodness sake, and she had conquered a warrior.

Chapter Seventeen

On the twenty-first day after her departure from Earth, Sharon, Liken, and Tair stood on the Shimerian side of the portal. They were waiting in line to transport back to Earth for the pledging ceremony. Tair glanced over his shoulder at the pactmates. Sharon was dressed in her pledge clothing. Her shimmering white halter was thin, and showed off her full breasts beautifully. Her white skirt stopped at mid-thigh calling attention to those wonderful legs. She certainly did not resemble any librarian Tair had ever seen.

Liken was in black, but his boots shone and he was wearing some expensive scent Tair could not identify. Tair studied the couple with great satisfaction. Sharon looked radiant and Liken could barely keep his eyes off of her. They were obviously happy. Sharon turned to him suddenly and said, "Tair, we need to talk." Her voice was serious.

Both men shuddered in instinctive dread at her words. Liken shot him a look of sympathy. Tair couldn't imagine what he had done. He couldn't keep the defensive note from his voice. "What is it, Sharon? Perhaps another time would be better to have this discussion?"

She wasn't being put off. "No, I don't think so. When are you planning to make Kate your pactmate?" It had been on her mind for some time.

The line moved forward. There was only one person ahead of them now. Tair shrugged and said, "She will be at your pledging today, will she not? It is an ideal time."

His casual gesture belied the depth of his real feelings. He was anxious to claim his pactmate. After seeing Liken and

Sharon together, especially this last week, he was eager to start his life with Kate.

Sharon nodded slowly. "Well, yes. But, don't you think I should talk to her first? Maybe explain a few things about Shimeria? It might smooth the way." *It might prevent major warfare* she wanted to say.

Tair smiled. "No. Absolutely not. She will learn as you did."

Sharon couldn't contain her doubt. Since she liked Tair and loved Kate like a sister, she wanted to spare both of them some of the pain and confusion she and Liken had gone through in the last few weeks. "She's a lot more...ummm...explosive than I am, Tair. I don't think her knowing period will be as easy as mine."

Tair laughed. "I am relying on it." He stepped through the portal and was gone.

Sharon turned to Liken, who was watching with an incredulous look on his face. "What?"

"Easy? Your knowing period was easy?" Sheer amazement permeated his voice.

She laughed. "Compared to Kate, believe me, I was easy."

Liken placed a hard kiss on her mouth. "Maybe they will be fortunate and find love as we have." Her eyes softened and he placed a tender hand on her cheek n response. She heard people in line behind them shifting restlessly. She turned and walked forward.

Grinning shamelessly, Liken waited until she was about to enter the portal. His voice echoed in the large room. "If not, a little interplanetary nookie won't kill them." The others in the line around them heard his words and laughed along with him.

Sharon couldn't help it. Men were always so sure of themselves. She laughed. "No, but Kate might." She was still laughing as she stepped into the portal and disappeared.

As he stepped through the portal on her heels, Liken thought about his soon-to-be pledgemate. He was very grateful she had agreed to make a life with him. His sweet librarian was beautiful, intelligent, and a fiery dream come to life. She was walking, talking love personified. She meant everything to him.

But, obviously, she did not know Tair. He felt the grin on his face grow wider. Sharon was going to be surprised again.

Of course, not as surprised as Kate...

Enjoy this excerpt from:
OATH OF CHALLENGE:
CONQUERING KATE

© Copyright Marly Chance 2002

All Rights Reserved, Ellora's Cave Publishing, Inc.

Prologue

The Shimerian population had been in trouble for many generations. There was a great disproportion of males and not enough female mates. Of the children born, a large percent were male. It was a downward spiral that spelled eventual extinction for an entire planet. Shimerian scientists worked feverishly to solve the mystery of the population problem, but were unsuccessful. As a temporary solution they proposed importing females from other planets or having males go off-planet for mates.

After listening to the scientists' grim reports, Shimerian government officials began to look for possible solutions. They studied other planets and concluded that Earth, with its many similarities, was a logical first choice.

Humans and Shimerians were similar biologically. The two planets were environmentally similar, although there were significant differences in atmosphere. However, these differences presented a major difficulty. Shimerians could not adapt well enough to the differences to live on Earth for longer than three weeks at a time. After three weeks they grew progressively sicker until death occurred.

Humans, on the other hand, were more adaptable. They were able to adjust to Shimerian atmosphere quickly and could live on the planet with no problem. Even more importantly, Shimerians and humans were biologically compatible enough to make interplanetary reproduction possible. A solution was in sight.

After lengthy negotiations, the Earth government agreed to help. The ShimEarth Friendship Treaty was signed. The Treaty was supposed to be the beginning of a new era in interplanetary cooperation for the greater good.

Earth agreed to provide potential mates for Shimerians. In return, Shimerian resources and technology were fully available to Earth. Already, in only the first eighty years since the signing, amazing cures for some of the worst Earth diseases had resulted from the cooperative knowledge provided by Shimerian scientists to Earth scientists.

However, the sharing of technology and culture was approached slowly and carefully. No one wanted conflict resulting from too rapid an integration. Each planet had its own secrets, but positive advances took place on both sides. Each government had its own reasons for ensuring success.

However, in the beginning, suspicion ran high. The Treaty was complicated to negotiate and even more difficult to implement. The Earth government, making clear it was not prostituting its women, agreed to provide a register of potential mates and carefully agreed upon Courtship Laws.

Since the Shimerian males' version of courtship leaned toward kidnapping and seduction, the Earth government had been very specific that the program would be voluntary and follow prescribed rules. Earth females chosen from the register or "called to Oath," were given three courtship or engagement options, two of which included a "knowing period."

If, after the knowing period and under certain conditions, the Earth female did not want to continue the union, she could file legal paperwork that the union was incompatible and should be dissolved. The third option was added in the event that a female had changed her mind. Basically, Earth officials tried to build in an escape clause. In the end, Shimeria was able to turn the clause to its advantage.

The register was considered by Earth to be similar to signing a contract with the armed services. Females signed and swore an oath to abide by the Oath contract. The penalties for breaking Oath were quite severe--imprisonment and heavy monetary fines. However, the social stigma of breaking Oath was considered much worse.

When the treaty had been signed some eighty years ago, there was hesitation by Earth females and only a few actually became Shimerian mates. However, as the positive breakthroughs in technology and medicine began to be widely felt, the Shimerian government pushed hard for a public relations program in higher learning centers to promote registering.

These "culture classes" explained the process in glowing terms and encouraged young women to register. The classes had a very idealistic slant with just enough excitement to entice. *"Help your fellow human beings and Shimerians, too,"* they persuaded, *"while having an adventure."*

More Earth females registered and were mated. Then, rumors began to surface about Shimerian men and their sexual abilities. Women spoke with sighs of their physical attributes, but a lot of information remained unknown. There was just enough mystery to intrigue and entice even the most hardheaded of women. More and more Earth females registered.

After a while, the overwhelming response meant that for every twenty thousand Earth women registered, only one would actually be called to Oath. Most would go on to fall in love with a man on Earth. When she married or at age thirty, her name would be removed from the register with thanks from her government for her willingness to serve.

Shimeria conducted its own educational campaign. Shimerian males were given "Earth culture classes" in school to understand the customs and the languages. In addition, more emphasis was placed on the importance of honing telepathic skills.

Shimerian males realized early that finding a mate was a difficult task. It involved years of telepathically probing and searching for their destined mate. When the male located his mate mentally, the odds were very good that she would be on the Earth register. If she was not on the register, there were other alternatives.

After all the years of practicing and searching, it was quite a moment for a Shimerian male to locate his mate. Some males went through their lifetime trying and not succeeding. No one could understand why some males located their mates at a particular time. It was a great mystery and a great source of frustration. Some called it luck. Some said chance. Some said destiny. And some said skill.

Some, like Tair da'Kamon considered it all of those things. Knowing Tair's skills, not many would dare to disagree. In the last few weeks, Tair's brother, Liken had called his mate to Oath. Rumor held that Tair had located his pactmate years ago, but had waited. Whisperers said he had been waiting for his brother to call his mate, so that Tair could be the couple's link. To be eligible to offer protection as a link, the male had to be unpledged at that time. Tair was very protective of his brother. Most felt the rumor could be entirely true.

Now that Liken was pledging with his mate and Tair was her link, many wondered if Tair would call his pactmate to Oath. Speculation was rife regarding his possible mate. He was a Guardian of exceptional skill, respected for his cunning and determination. What kind of Earth female would be a match for such a warrior?

Tair heard the new rumors and arched an eyebrow in sardonic amusement. As usual, he kept his own counsel. He never confirmed or denied anything. Gossipmongers were left to wonder. However, later in private, Tair did not bother hiding his lusty smile of anticipation. Indeed, he had found his mate. Her name was Kate...

Chapter 1

Men, Kate concluded, are pretty much like an expensive pair of stockings -- sexy when you first try them on, but apt to run like hell at the first snag. Leaning back in her chair, she sighed and waved a mental goodbye to Todd.

He had been an amusing lover and a nice diversion from the drudgery of her heavy work schedule. It was a shame that he had to disappear and take her good sex life with him. Truthfully, she rather thought she'd miss the sex more than Todd.

Suddenly, a deep masculine voice broke her train of thought. "I've heard that sigh before. It can only mean trouble."

Kate smiled with surprised pleasure. "I'm not the troublemaker in this family, remember? Gage, what are you doing here?"

Gage strolled into her office and sat down with unconscious masculine grace. Kate assessed her brother silently. He was six foot, three with blond hair and blue eyes. Muscular and athletic, he had an easy charm to match.

Under the movie star good looks, though, he looked tired. She could see traces of strain in his face, and there was a lurking sadness in those crystal blue eyes. Frowning with concern, she continued, "And why do you look so sad?"

Gage rolled his eyes, though affectionately. "Men do not get sad, Kate. Women get sad. Men get pissed off. And I'm not either of those things. I'm fine. You're the one sighing. What's the sigh all about?"

Kate stared hard at him a moment, but knew he wouldn't be budged. He wasn't going to tell her until he was ready. She didn't like seeing that look on his face at all. She could guess why it was there, and the mere thought sent a touch of panic through her veins.

Her brother would not die. She would fight fate, or God, or whomever she had to fight, but she was not losing Gage. Pasting a determined smile on her face, she said lightly, "I could be sighing at the thought of the chocolate ice cream I had at lunch."

Gage threw back his head and laughed. Shaking his head at her, he said, "First of all, you don't like ice cream. A horrible sin, but it's true. Secondly, knowing you, you probably worked right through lunch. Unless you lunched with, uhhh what's the name this time? Was it Brad or Brent?"

Kate gave him a cold glare designed to freeze the blood in his veins. "It was neither. Do try to keep up. His name was Todd. And he's outlived his usefulness as of this morning."

Gage's expression sobered a little, but the amusement was still in his voice. "Poor bastard. What did you do? Tell him he was fired without further notice? Oh, I know, you're both lawyers. You sent him papers addressed to 'Dumpee.'"

Kate forced a rather brittle laugh and nearly winced. "Actually, I believe I received the papers this time. But, no doubt he'd have received some from me soon enough."

Gage sat up and searched her face with suddenly gentle eyes. "Kate, are you okay? Did you really care about this one?"

Kate sighed and felt a pang of sadness that had nothing to do with Todd. "No, actually, I didn't. I mean, I cared about him as a person, but you know me–I don't develop lasting relationships."

Gage shook his head. "That's not true and you know it. Look at you and Sharon. You've been friends for forever. "

Kate went cold with icy dread at the mention of Sharon. Taking a deep breath, she said with resignation, "Sharon. That's right. You don't know about Sharon."

Looking really alarmed now, Gage asked, "What's happened?"

Kate met his eyes squarely. "Sharon was called to Oath. She's due back from Shimeria today. I have the incompatibility papers already drawn up for her signature. "

Gage eyes widened in shock. "Called to Oath? Sharon?" He looked dazed at the thought. "Sharon is so…"

He fell silent, obviously trying to think of a term. "And Shimerians are so…"

Kate smiled grimly. "Yes, exactly. If they've harmed her in any way, I'll go there myself and see justice done. I swear I will."

Thoughts of her sheltered librarian best friend in the arms of a dominant, sexually aggressive alien had given Kate quite a few sleepless nights in the last three weeks. Thank God Sharon was coming home today. She would see her and make sure everything was okay. Feeling a familiar sense of frustration at her inability to do anything now, she focused on explaining the specifics to Gage.

"His name is Liken da'Kamon. He invoked the Oath three weeks ago and Sharon chose Seduction." Her mind filled with images of herself and Sharon at eighteen, so young and idealistic, signing the register. Wincing at the thought of how she'd urged Sharon to sign, she felt a fresh wave of guilt and helplessness.

Gage knew he looked outwardly composed. He'd had a lifetime of hiding his emotions, even from his sister. But inside he was truly shocked and worried at the news. Straightening his shoulders, he asked precisely, "What do you mean she chose Seduction?"

Kate heard the dangerous edge to his voice and said quietly, "Earth females get three options as to the Oath the Shimerian male will make: Seduction, Challenge, or Capture."

Gage tried to remember what he could about Shimeria. It wasn't much. He had met some Shimerian males in his travels, but he'd never been off-planet to visit the place. The males whom he'd met were big and lusty types, powerfully built and aggressively male. He couldn't imagine Sharon with that kind of man.

He felt a growing anger at the thought of what might have happened to Sharon. Focusing on getting as much information as possible, he said shortly, "Explain the options to me. What exactly happens?"

Kate watched the growing anger in her brother and felt a little relieved. They would help Sharon together. Taking another deep, calming breath, she said, "I've been going over the paperwork carefully. If the female chooses Seduction, she goes to Shimeria with him for three weeks referred to as a "knowing period." He gets certain intimacies at certain times progressively."

She realized she was tapping her fingers impatiently on the desk out of sheer nerves and stopped immediately. "Total intimacy occurs within three days. Basically, he takes an oath to seduce her into staying with him. After three weeks, if he's successful, they have a pledge ceremony and go back to Shimeria to live. If he's unsuccessful in convincing her to stay at the end of the knowing period, she can file incompatible papers and dissolve the pact."

Gage tensed even more and said shortly, "Couldn't she have picked one of the other options?"

Kate sighed. "Believe me, for Sharon that would have been worse. The Oath of Challenge is similar to the Seduction Oath. The female agrees to cooperate sexually with any intimacy for two weeks--except intercourse. Obviously, he can't abuse her or force her into repulsive acts. He's challenging her to explore her sexuality without giving in to total intimacy."

The words came out huskier than she intended. Clearing her throat, she continued, "If she has intercourse with him, she is ineligible to file for noncomp. She has to pledge with him and stay."

Kate felt a little warm at the discussion of the Challenge Oath. Despite her worry for Sharon, she couldn't help feeling intrigued at the thought. What would it be like to explore your desires in that way?

An image of a Liken's broad-shouldered brother flashed through her mind. There was something about him. He kept popping into her thoughts. She had even awakened from a few rather interesting dreams. She might see him today when she went to the Pactbuilding to see Sharon and file the papers. Immediately, she banished the thought.

With each sentence, Gage could feel his blood pressure rising. "And Capture?"

Shrugging helplessly, Kate explained, "In my opinion, it's the most dangerous of the three. The female runs and tries to evade the male for a month. She has two advantages: she gets a 24-hour head-start and Shimerians can only stay on Earth for three weeks without getting ill. The illness progresses rapidly and is fatal if they don't return to their own world. They can't adjust to our atmosphere."

She wearily rubbed the back of her neck where it had begun to ache. "I wish we couldn't adjust to their atmosphere, but we can."

Gage felt guilt all the way down to his toes. He had been unavailable and out of touch when his family needed him. He felt the guilt turn to anger at his own selfishness. He should have been there for them.

He said, "I'm sorry, Kate. The two of you should have been able to come to me. I would have helped hide her. He wouldn't have found her. And if he had, he wouldn't have taken her away."

Kate smiled and shook her head. "Gage, as much as I appreciate the protectiveness, we could have handled it ourselves. Besides, she couldn't break Oath. Signing the register is legally binding. She would have faced imprisonment here. She could have run under the Capture option, but…"

She leaned back in her chair and said grimly, "We couldn't risk the consequences if she was caught. If the male captures her, she has to obey him sexually for however much of the month is left. He can do what he likes to her, as long as he doesn't hurt her emotionally or physically."

Seeing the hardness in her brother's eyes, she forced a more neutral tone. "A high stakes gamble with possibly intense sexual consequences. For Sharon, it was out of the question. Oh, and with Capture, noncomp papers are out, too. You're stuck."

Gage leaned back in his chair and wiped his hand over his face in an absent-minded gesture of frustration. Obviously, Sharon had made the only choice that she could make, given the options. Suddenly, he remembered something else about Shimerians. He hated to even mention the topic to Kate. She would get upset, but he had to know. "They're psychic, aren't they? Or some form of it?"

Kate knew her face had gone pale at the mention of the word, but she said evenly, "Yes, I think they have some unusual mental abilities. I couldn't find any concrete evidence in my research, but there are too many rumors from too many places." She looked away.

Gage felt the weight of silence hang between them for a long moment. Kate was avoiding looking at him. He decided to confront the issue directly. "Kate, we both know psychic powers are possible. I'm clairvoyant and there's no getting around it. I've proven it enough times in our lives. Just because you don't like what I see, doesn't mean it's not real."

Panic and anger raged inside her, so Kate purposefully turned cool. "It's not that I don't believe in your powers. You know I do. I just don't believe in destiny. You may have seen your…" her voice caught, but she quickly got it under control, "…death, but I refuse to accept it. You're healthy and sitting right here in front of me. Nothing's going to happen."

Gage's heart twisted at the look on his sister's face. She knew deep down that he was right, but she couldn't accept it. Unfortunately, she was going to have to accept it soon. He could sense time running out.

There was a new feeling of urgency lately. The vision was occurring with an alarming frequency now. He had hoped he was overstressed and that a vacation would lessen the feeling and the dreams. Instead, as he'd relaxed, they'd only grown stronger. He could feel his life slipping away, hour by hour. His heart sped up in his chest. Not much longer. There was no doubt.

Watching Kate's pain-filled face, he groped helplessly with a way to comfort her. Pasting on a smile he said lightly, "Come on, Kit-Kate, you know I've lived a life full enough for ten men."

He watched with rising panic as her eyes grew over-bright at the childhood nickname. Kate never cried. This conversation was getting bad in a hurry. Deliberately goading her he said, "Hey, I've single-handedly worked my way through the female population of this city and two foreign cities as well. I don't plan to die until I have at least two more cities under my belt."

Kate knew what he was doing. He was bringing up his playboy image to distract her. Rather than being distracted, she spoke with firm resolve. "I don't care what visions you've had. You're not dying young and that's final." Attempting to lighten the moment, she continued primly, "And psychic visions are no excuse for being oversexed."

Gage couldn't help admiring his sister's determination and control. Kate was one hell of a fighter. He grinned. "Who needs an excuse for being oversexed when it's so much fun?"

Suddenly, there was a loud commotion in the hallway. Gage stood and flashed a warning look at Kate. "Stay here. Something's happening."

Kate ignored her brother and stood as well. Suddenly, the flustered voice of her assistant was heard saying clearly, "But sirs, you can't interrupt her. Ms. Carson is busy. If you'll just allow me to…"

Two hulking Pactreps entered her office, with her worried assistant right behind them murmuring objections and apologies. Seeing Gage tense, she moved quickly to bring things under control. She nodded to her assistant. "Darren, it's okay. I'm willing to see these two *gentlemen.*" She placed a sarcastic emphasis on the last word.

Gage arched an eyebrow at her in question. She shook her head slightly and dropped casually into her chair. She watched as Gage moved over to the left, and leaned against the wall. He crossed his arms over his chest. He looked at the Pactreps like a sleepy tiger deciding lazily when to pounce on his meal.

Her assistant backed out of the office with an apologetic look. The Pactreps came to a halt in front of her desk. They were wearing identical black pants and white shirts. They were easily six feet, six inches tall and heavily muscled. They looked more like bodyguards than government paper servers.

Gage watched the change come over his sister. When she leaned back in her chair, eyes glinting like ice, smiling wickedly, he almost felt sorry for the Pactreps. When Kate had that look, there was always hell to pay.

She crossed one leg over the other and said gaily, "Hello, boys. It's been weeks since I saw you last, hasn't it?"

Gage could see the huge men flinch a little and had to stifle an urge to laugh. This was going to be good. When neither man responded, Gage realized it was going to be *really* good.

They seemed to be gathering their courage. Considering his sister was five feet six inches tall and less than half of either of their body weights, the sight of the two hesitant reps was hilarious.

Finally, they had shown up to take her to Sharon, Kate thought gleefully. Her dealings with the Pact Officials this week had been unproductive. Basically, they had succeeded in convincing her that she would be contacted when Sharon was due to arrive. Any other information she requested was met with bureaucratic jargon and evasion.

Now, she had the same two Pacteps assigned to escort her as last time. When the reps remained silent, she gave them a mocking look. They remembered her well. Good. She arched one smooth eyebrow and said overly pleasantly, "Oh, dear. I'm speaking too fast for you again, aren't I?"

Speaking slowly and carefully, as if to a small child, she said, "Now, what were your names? Oh yes, Everest and Rushmore. Couldn't get me to come to you, so you had to come to me?"

One of the men spoke. "I'm Pactrepresentative Dik si'Dalon and this is Jr. Pactrep Joseph Swann."

Kate nearly broke into laughter at the incongruity of the last name Swann. The rep was a huge hulking creature, and graceful he was not. Of course, he didn't look like anybody's junior anything either. Struggling to keep a straight face, she said, "Let's not make molehills out of mountains, shall we?"

When their faces remained blank, she sighed. Suddenly changing tactics, she demanded in a hard voice, "What do you want? And you'd better not be telling me Sharon is being kept past today. I've read the paperwork and my client will *not* be forcibly detained."

The two men glanced at each other and then Swann spoke in a cautious voice. "Sharon Glaston is returning today. We have the witness order to summon you there. The pledging ceremony is to be held at three o'clock."

Kate sat up, uncrossed her legs, and placed her hands on her desk. In her coldest voice, she challenged, "The hell it will. I notice you're just now notifying me and it's already two-fifteen. Left it a little late there, didn't you Junior?"

He winced, but held his ground. "We are here to notify you of the pledge ceremony and your required presence. In addition, we have more papers to serve."

Taking a step toward Gage, Swann approached him and said, "We have been searching for you. You are her brother, correct?"

Gage watched the man through narrowed eyes. Something was going on here, and he had a sudden feeling it involved Kate and not Sharon. Straightening from the wall, he said coolly, "Yes, I'm Gage Carson. Why?"

The man handed Gage a piece of paper gingerly, as if he was feeding a wild animal. When Gage took the paper, Swann stepped back cautiously. Gage began reading.

Kate watched her brother's brow wrinkle in confusion. As his head came up in surprise, he shot her a stunned look she couldn't interpret. "What is it?" she asked in alarm.

Pactrep si'Dalon stepped in front of her. Suddenly realizing the two men were between her and her brother, she stepped forward until she was within a foot of si'Dalon and glared up at him.

The representative held up another sheet of paper and began to read. "Katherine Harmony Carson," his voice nearly choked on her middle name, but he continued reading in a low steady voice. "You are hereby summoned to Oath by the world government of Shimeria and the..."

"What?!" Kate knew her voice was shrill, but she was shocked to the core. "Did you just say *I've* been summoned to Oath?!"

The representative continued reading as if his very mission in life was to finish the summons. "...and the United Government of..." Gage and Kate began talking at the same time.

"No way in hell," Gage said in a dangerously furious voice. "She's not going. You guys have picked the wrong two women. I'm telling you now--it's not happening."

Kate continued exclaiming, "There is no way that could be right. Do you know what the odds of Sharon and my both being summoned are? Only one in twenty thousand on the register is summoned. The odds of two best friends being called are astronomical. Somebody has screwed up here big time."

Suddenly she heard a familiar name in the midst of the rep's droning. "Wait a second. Did you say the name Tair da'Kamon? As in--a relative of Liken da'Kamon?"

Her mind filled again with the image of the Shimerian male, Liken's brother whom she had met briefly at Sharon's pact ceremony. She knew down to her bones he was the one. His drop-dead good looks were exceeded only by his arrogance.

Remembering his smugly grinning face, she had the sudden impulse to hit something, *hard*. He had known while they were talking that he would summon her to Oath. That knowing light in his eyes and smug attitude made sense now. She felt fury flood her at the mere thought.

The Pactrep's voice stopped finally as he reached the end of the summons. Looking up, he said in a gloating voice, "It is done. You must accompany us to the Pactbuilding for the ceremony." His entire body went tense as if he expected her to spring at him.

Kate's eyelids came down to hide her eyes and her face lost all expression. With a narrow look, she said calmly, "I'll meet you boys there."

Gage made a sudden motion forward, but her pointed look stopped him in his tracks. Studying his sister, he knew she had developed a plan. Deciding to trust her for the moment, he said casually, "I'll transport you."

Both Pactreps shook their heads. Swann said, "You both must accompany us now. It is in the papers."

Kate reached out and took the paper from si'Dalon. Reading it over carefully, she found the clause. He was right. Thinking hard for a minute, she said flatly, "I'll accompany you. We'll notify my partners of what's happening and drop by my house first."

Suddenly, she realized that Sharon would be getting back shortly. Her temper spiked as she realized the timing. She clamped down swiftly on her anger yet again and said coolly, "Or not. I guess you guys have timed it so that I have to leave with you to meet Sharon. Very clever, boys. I never would have suspected an active brain cell between the two of you. Well done."

Swann ignored the insult. "All notifications will be made and procedures followed. The Pactmakers will take care of any necessary details while you are on Shimeria. Everything from plant and pet care to bills to family and work explanations will be handled diligently. You have nothing to fear."

It was the wrong word choice. Kate's back stiffened and she said coldly, "Oh, I'm not afraid. I'm looking forward to having a discussion with Tair. Let's go."

She picked up a stack of papers off her desk and removed her purse from a drawer. She put the papers in her purse with calm efficiency. Slinging it over her shoulder and flashing the two Pactreps a look of disdain, she walked out of the room without a backward glance.

Gage watched his sister walk around the Pactrep and out the door with regal grace and felt like cheering. He knew she had to be panicked at the thought of being summoned, but it didn't show. She had decided to focus her energies on Tair. He knew that sharp brain of hers was busy plotting and planning. Well, he had a few plots of his own. First things first, however.

As Pactrep si'Dilon left in Kate's wake, Gage turned to find Swann regarding him warily. Gage said, "Enjoy your moment of triumph. Kate will be stirring up hell soon enough." Leaning forward until he was within inches of touching the representative, he said, "Of course, you're probably not afraid. Kate has some scruples. She won't blame you for this mess. She knows you're just doing your job."

Gage smiled and grabbed Swann's shirt. He stared hard into the other man's eyes, watching Swann's face grow pale in response. He kept his voice low and even as he continued, "I, on the other hand, don't give a damn about scruples."

He released the man's shirt and leaned back. He said matter-of-factly, "Fuck scruples. Whoever hurts them will pay no matter how small their part in this scheme. If Sharon or Kate suffers, there's no planet in existence where you'll ever be safe." He stepped around the Pactrep and strolled out of the office.

Swann stood there a moment in the silence of the room. The icy threat he had seen in those eyes had been chilling. He knew Gage's background. He felt like he had escaped death by an inch. With absolute certainty he knew Gage's words were true. He sighed.

Some men, he reflected, were like cobras. If you tangled with them, one of you most likely ended up dead. There were days when his job really sucked. With weary steps, he moved to follow the others. Government servants never got any respect.

About the author:

Award-winning erotic romance author Marly Chance lives in a small Tennessee town where truth is always stranger than fiction. She believes firmly in happy endings, chocolate, and good friends.

She is one of the bestselling authors at Ellora's Cave Publishing and was honored with the Ellora's Cave Publisher's Choice Award for 2002.

Marly welcomes mail from readers. You can write to her c/o Ellora's Cave Publishing at 1337 Commerce Drive, Suite 13, Stow OH 44224.

Also by Marly Chance:

Oath of Challenge: Conquering Kate
A Wish Away *Wicked Wishes anthology*
Deadline

Why an electronic book?

We live in the Information Age—an exciting time in the history of human civilization in which technology rules supreme and continues to progress in leaps and bounds every minute of every hour of every day. For a multitude of reasons, more and more avid literary fans are opting to purchase e-books instead of paperbacks. The question to those not yet initiated to the world of electronic reading is simply: *why?*

1. *Price.* An electronic title at Ellora's Cave Publishing runs anywhere from 40-75% less than the cover price of the <u>exact same title</u> in paperback format. Why? Cold mathematics. It is less expensive to publish an e-book than it is to publish a paperback, so the savings are passed along to the consumer.

2. *Space.* Running out of room to house your paperback books? That is one worry you will never have with electronic novels. For a low one-time cost, you can purchase a handheld computer designed specifically for e-reading purposes. Many e-readers are larger than the average handheld, giving you plenty of screen room. Better yet, hundreds of titles can be stored within your new library—a single microchip. (Please note that Ellora's Cave does not endorse any specific brands. You can check our website at www.ellorascave.com for customer recommendations we make available to new consumers.)

3. *Mobility.* Because your new library now consists of only a microchip, your entire cache of books can be taken with you wherever you go.

4. *Personal preferences are accounted for.* Are the words you are currently reading too small? Too large?

Too...**ANNOYING**? Paperback books cannot be modified according to personal preferences, but e-books can.

5. *Innovation.* The way you read a book is not the only advancement the Information Age has gifted the literary community with. There is also the factor of what you can read. Ellora's Cave Publishing will be introducing a new line of interactive titles that are available in e-book format only.

6. *Instant gratification.* Is it the middle of the night and all the bookstores are closed? Are you tired of waiting days—sometimes weeks—for online and offline bookstores to ship the novels you bought? Ellora's Cave Publishing sells instantaneous downloads 24 hours a day, 7 days a week, 365 days a year. Our e-book delivery system is 100% automated, meaning your order is filled as soon as you pay for it.

Those are a few of the top reasons why electronic novels are displacing paperbacks for many an avid reader. As always, Ellora's Cave Publishing welcomes your questions and comments. We invite you to email us at service@ellorascave.com or write to us directly at: 1337 Commerce Drive, Suite 13, Stow OH 44224.

Printed in the United States
56411LVS00002B